MW00571599

Tales of the Troupe

A COLLECTION OF SHORT STORIES BY

ROB DINSMOOR

Zingology Press: For your publishing needs

www.zingologypress.com

ISBN 1448644070

To order additional copes of this book, contact:
Zingology Press
www.zingologypress.com
info@zingology.com

To Mom, my first editor

Acknowledgments

I thank the following people: the group of wonderful writers and performers who comprised a group, coincidentally called Chucklehead and people who gave me invaluable feedback on the manuscript, including Amy Bishop, Carol Bistrong, Elisabeth Clark, Linda Finnigan, Beth Foley, Beth Hogan, Eleanor Lodge, Dorothy Stephens, and Tina Varinos; my friends and family members (including ex-wife) who supported me in my writing career; and Zingology Press, for offering me the opportunity to put this book in print.

TABLE OF CONTENTS

WHO'S WHO IN THE TROUPE

Artistic Director
Dirk

Musical Director
Jim

Video Czar
Paul

Performers
Dirk
Pat
Rick
Angie (Jim's girlfriend)
Rose
Spanky

Writers
Rob
Peter
Judy
Russell

PROLOGUE

I have just completed my third frame, executing my third strike in a row, and am on my third beer, and life is good. I am in the alcohol "zone." I am the Master.

It is the autumn of 1986. I am surrounded by my new family, my troupe. We have only recently discovered this hidden bowling alley. There is a less-than-blazing sign out front that says "Bowling" and you take a rickety old elevator, with an iron gate and an authentic elevator man, to the third floor, and up there you find eight bowling lanes miraculously crammed inside an unlikely-looking small room.

It is about six months after a *Vogue* headline announced "They'll Take Manhattan"–referring to Chucklehead, our comedy troupe of six performers and four writers–and we believe it. We go everywhere together. Whenever one of us gets invited to a party, all of us come, see, and conquer. We show up together and instantly parties go from nervous small-talk to wild gesticulating and insane laughter. We leave when the booze runs out, and then the party is over, for all practical purposes.

There are a bunch of us there that night. There are the troupe's performers: the gay, manic and sometimes in-your-face Rick; the beautiful, wonderfully sleazy but generally elusive Angie; her boyfriend Jim, who composes and plays the show's music and laughs like an evil elf whenever anything goes wrong; Brooklyn-born Pat, who runs a mail-order company selling comic books, warrior babe posters, and soft-core pornography books that border on good taste; Dirk, the artistic director, whose California laid-back manner belies a ruthlessly competitive soul; beautiful Rose, who could morph her face into a grotesque Mardi Gras mask at will, and Spanky, half ladies' man, half toddler, who once wore a pair of shorts—and no underpants—an entire day before noticing a big tear down the back.

And there are the writers: the affable but back-stabbing Russell and me, the compulsive and repressed souse, who have distinguished myself as a real party animal in a group that prides itself on substance abuse. Paul, our video czar, as always, takes video home movies whenever the troupe gets together, as if the footage might some day be worth something. That night we are missing two writers—Peter, who as a kid had appeared as a ventriloquist on "To Tell the Truth," and Judy, at once totally hip and totally above the whole idea of being hip.

We are still in our late twenties and life is good. The troupe has yet to disband. I have yet to be married and divorced, yet to even meet my future bride. We're all still alive. And at that precise moment in time, we are completely in love with being us.

That night, as most nights with the troupe, and even most nights in general, has become a blur for me. By the fourth frame I have just the right levels of serotonin and dopamine in my brain to feel absolutely invincible, and when I send the ball down the alley, all of the pins obligingly go down. "The Master!" Jim calls out, since I always bowl better after a couple of drinks.

The two lanes we've commandeered can only seat six of us, so while we aren't bowling, we're at the bar/lunch counter drinking our beers. There I help form the wall of flesh that was already made up of Rick, Spanky, Ken, and Angie. Rick's cigarette is cocked upward in his mouth and he is kind of squinting. Angie's luscious lips are kissing the end of a cigarette, too, and when she leans into Ken's ear to be heard, her smoke blows smoke right into his face, and while Ken doesn't smoke, he doesn't seem to mind at all. I order another Bud from the lady behind the counter, get it, and turn to engulf myself in the group.

Almost immediately, someone taps me on the shoulder. It is my turn. I hand my beer to Angie, saying, "Guard this for me, will you?" and as I step away, she is drinking it and making it her own.

Dismissively, I grab the first ball my hands came to, chuck it down the alley and, as expected, it is a strike. In unison, now, Jim, Remy, Rose, Russell, and Dirk raise their fists and chant, "The Master!"

Waving away their mock adoration, I say, "Just call me again when it's my turn."

Since Angie is now sucking down the last of my beer, I get another one and join the mob again. They are all laughing loudly now, and I am hoping to be able to pick up a line and reel in the joke, but I never do. It is because I'm already somewhat hard of hearing but don't really know it yet. Angie is now strategically placed, and I can rest my arm easily across her back, and I find myself strangely transfixed by her earring, and her left buttock is pressed firmly against the crotch of my jeans. Occasionally she rests her head on my shoulder and grabs a gulp of my beer. I am having a very hard time now making out any of the conversation that is going on, but it doesn't matter–I'm in Heaven.

When The Master is summoned for his sixth frame, he leaves the huddle with mixed feelings. It is another strike, and when I approach the alley for the seventh frame, Dirk, Remy, and Jim are prostrate on the floor, bowing like Muslims toward the Mecca. "The Master! The Master! The Master!"

I stumble up to the edge of the lane and slide the ball more or less forward. It starts off pointed slightly to the left of center, looks like it will wind up in the gutter, veers to the right toward the center pin and then winds up knocking off only four pins on the right side. When I turn to face my adorers, they are standing there dumbstruck. My second ball takes exactly the same trajectory as the first and rolls easily through the hole the first one has so conveniently provided.

I know then that I am way past my optimal alcohol "zone" and that the rest of my game will consist of gutter balls and swearing. I go back to the counter mob where Ken has placed himself strategically on the outside of Angie so he can have her all to himself.

LARGER THAN LIFE

The Westbeth Theatre is so incredibly far west that you can actually see the Hudson River from its front door. To get there, you just go west from the hustle and bustle of Sixth Avenue, west past the narrow, twisty side streets lined with tiny Italian restaurants in a haze of garlic, west past the endless parade of leather queens on Christopher Street, until you get to a few blocks of quiet brownstones. On a warm summer night, a breeze comes off the River, carrying a scent that is deeply intoxicating but not altogether wholesome.

That summer night in 1984, Natasha and I walked arm in arm down the street toward the theatre, slightly giddy on each other and the Thai dinner we'd just had in the Village. "So, how do you know this guy again?" she asked.

"My junior year at Dartmouth, this guy from Cornell named Sol Greenberg decided to start a consortium of humor magazines from different schools, stretching out across the United States."

"And Dirk was part of that consortium?"

"No. When I moved to New York, Sol got in touch with me because he wanted us to pool our talents on a parody of college textbooks. I became the assistant editor of that. It never came out. Sol lost interest in it and dropped it.

"But that's when I met Dirk, who had edited the Stanford Chaparral and I wasn't particularly impressed with him. He showed up at one our textbook editorial meetings all high and giggling."

"But you still kept in touch?"

"No. One day I was at a bar in SoHo called Sweeps when a tap came on my shoulder and it was Dirk. He recognized me and said he was doing this stand-up act and would I like to come down and see it? He could comp me in. I wasn't expecting much, but I said sure.

"Well, most of the guys down there were these total bone-heads who swore a lot, but then Dirk came on in this three-piece suit and looking like this crazed and repressed super-honkie, and he was just hysterical! Then he brought out this mop-haired piano player and started singing these frenetic songs about caffeine and middle-management angst, and it wasn't just funny, it's enervating. I don't think I've ever seen anything so hip and funny and cool."

"He sounds like quite a character," she said, and I found my left eye squinting just slightly at the way she said it.

I had never loved any woman more deeply, but certain things she said were starting to irritate me. Just a little. We had become romantically involved eight months ago at the American Diabetes Association, where I worked as an editor and proofread-er and she was an administrative assistant in Human Resources. She was everything I wanted in a woman—cute, intelligent, reliable, good-hearted, and level-headed. Together we had a secret life together that none of our co-workers even suspected. We kept our cool when other people were around, but little notes would mys-teriously appear in the top drawer of each others' desks: "Tasha–Can I kidnap you tonight and do unspeakable things to you?–Clark Kent." "You betcha, my Man of Steel!"

I was deeply grateful to her because she was only the sec-ond woman in my life who had ever consented to sleep with me. But every so often, she would ask questions about where I saw the two of us in five years and other equally morbid stuff. We had our whole lives ahead of us. Why ruin it with plans?

"Why is it you've never talked about any of these people?" she asked.

"I guess I fell out of touch with them a while back," I said, trying to hide my sadness. Eight months, to be exact.

We came to the theatre, an unassuming concrete structure abutting an apartment building and a basketball court. Just inside the door of the theatre was a box office window, where a sleazy-looking guy with a mustache in his early twenties sold us our tickets and gave us our programs, which were typewritten, photo-copied on color stock, and stapled together. We went up the drab staircase to the somewhat drab cinderblock lobby.

Posters of old shows at the Westbeth decorated the walls. I had actually been to one or two very low-budget, very unusual, utterly fascinating plays there, and recognized the posters for them. The rest of them could have come from another planet.

About 15 other people were milling around the lobby. Like any uncomfortable theatre-goers, we sat and read the program several times as if the information were all very important. Then I tucked my copy into the small copy of Jack London's *Call of the Wild*, which I was carrying around in my back pocket at the time.

All together, there were eight cast members. "I recognize Dirk, and his piano player is Jim, but I don't know who all these other people are," I confessed to Natasha.

When the usher let us in, I saw that the space was fairly typical of off-off Broadway Theatre–that is, tiny. Inside the dark, hot, dusty room were four rows of two columns of five folding chairs arranged on a platform with four small tiers. The smell of sawdust was in the air. Natasha's eyes widened. The last thing we had gone to see together was "Cats."

Unlike a Broadway show, here there was no predicting what it would be like. It could be an amazing play. It could be a piece of crap. It could be an amazing piece of crap. Among us 25 audience members, there was sort of a shared anxiousness of not knowing. Going to a seedy little theatre like this one was akin to what I imagined it would have been like to visit a speakeasy in the 1920s. The cast and audience were conspiring to create a little secret society with rules of our own.

Every so often, I had ventured into one of these off-off Broadway productions at the prodding of some friend or co-worker, only to watch two or three actors in turtlenecks mime and pontificate their way through two-hour sensory deprivation experiments. Audience members would sit patiently in these folding metal torture chairs, flex their feet to avoid calf cramps, stifle their yawns, applaud politely at the end, stay long enough to show the actor or playwright that they did their duty by attending, and then retreat before having to lie convincingly about how good the show was. I hoped this wasn't one of those.

Snazzy music from a synthesizer blasted over the speakers. The lights came up on some sort of South American native pulling tourists through the jungle on an enormous cart. It wasn't one of these jungles painted on a backdrop begging the audience to be taken seriously. There were solid vines, albeit made of plastic, that the actors had to constantly push their way through. They were singing a song about being in paradise. And so "Island Paradise" began.

During this first musical number, as the tourists were arriving, Natasha began to giggle. That was a good sign. "What is it?" I whispered.

"I really like the fat guy in the Hawaiian shirt!" she said. "He's so cute!"

I could immediately spot the fat guy to whom she was referring. I had him clocked at about 300 pounds. But I saw the appeal. He had these shining, expressive eyes, soft cheeks, and an expansive, innocent smile, like some enormous baby bundle of joy. Where did he find this guy? I wondered. Did he put in a casting call for "Adorable Fat Guy?"

Dirk was playing the sleazy owner of a resort situated in an unstable South or Latin American dictatorship. Near the beginning he is complaining to the local general, a tall dark man with slick black hair, that his death squad is performing its executions too close to the tennis courts and that members have been complaining about the noise. It was an excellent premise, Dirk was good in his role, and I had no idea where he got his Latin American general.

The second musical number was something called, "Casual Sex," in which Dirk was fondling, straddling, leapfrogging with, and everything short of dry humping two of the most beautiful women I'd ever seen in real life, dressed in bikinis. One of them was this curvy, breezy blonde with a sensually fleshy butt, dripping with brattiness and superior attitude. The other was a veritable *Penthouse* Pet of the Month—a dark-haired petite but busty Jewish or Italian girl with a sort of aggressive, in-your-face sexuality. That lucky sonofabitch. I wondered if he was sleeping with either one of them or both. God, I hated my stupid little desk job.

"That's a pretty cheap laugh, if you ask me," Natasha whispered. Though I disagreed, I nodded just to shut her up.

As the plot thickened, we met one of the rebel soldiers, a huge, muscular Latin American monster of a man with a painted face, camouflage clothes, a headband, and a machine gun. Where did he find these people? Dirk's sleazy character began to play both ends of this civil war, making deals with the general first and then the rebels.

When the musical ended, the 25 of us in the audience stood and applauded. What we lacked in numbers, we made up for in enthusiasm. The cast members took their curtain calls, and then the lights came up in the audience. Natasha started heading for the door, but I held her back. "I should really stay and pay my respects to Dirk," I said.

I waited around briefly for him to show up in the front of the theater. Then I saw a red-haired woman about my age just barge on back stage and decided to follow her. It turns out she was approaching the gorgeous brunette Jewish/Italian woman, who was wearing only a teal bra or bikini top and was in the process of struggling to pull up a pair of very tight jeans. Sweat ran down her face in tiny beads and dripped onto her soft, supple breasts, and she gave off a tangy odor of sweat mixed with the sweet, creamy scent of base make-up. She twisted and pulled the denim, trying to force it up over her tight, jiggling teal-clad buns, but was having such trouble, probably because the sweat was making the denim cling.

The redhead hugged her and said, "I just wanted to stop backstage and say, great show, honey! You were marvelous!"

"Thanks, Rose! It was so sweet of you to come!" the actress answered. She turned and pulled her rich, tan abdomen up and inward, making her breasts press forward, and quickly managed to slide the button through its hole. As she squatted, making a lethal parabolic curve with her buns, and then forcefully pulled up on the zipper, I noticed things had gotten strangely quiet. I looked up from her zipper to see that she and the redhead were now staring at me.

My head jerked back just slightly and nonchalance took over my demeanor, but my nostrils were still flaring. "Hi!" she said, with the congeniality of a hostess.

I frowned and then put on my best poker face. "Do you know Dirk's whereabouts?" I asked very soberly.

The redhead turned to me, wide-eyed, taunting me like a third-grade bully. "Why? What's he done, officer?"

The brunette gave her a disciplinary whack on the shoulder. "I don't know where Dirk is. He probably stepped out to have a butt," she said, and smiled again. "Did you like the show?"

I assumed she meant the musical, and not the reverse striptease. "Oh, I loved it. Great satire. And I really liked that musical number you did with Dirk. It was–It was a great show! You were so–You were great!"

"Thanks!" she said. "How do you know Dirk?"

"I was editor of the Dartmouth Jack O'Lantern when he was editor of the Stanford Chaparral," I said, as if answering a question on a job interview. "So, obviously, we go back a few years."

"Obviously."

"So, how do you know Dirk?" I asked.

"From the musical," she said, nodding.

"That makes sense."

"Actually, my boyfriend knows Dirk, and he got me in the show."

A silence hung in the air for a few seconds, and I finally broke it. "Well, carry on. I'm going to go on a hunting expedition for Dirk."

"Hope you bag him!" the redhead said.

As I stepped back out into the theatre, I saw Natasha sitting in one of the folding chairs, her feet flat on the floor, fanning herself with the program. "Did you find your friend?"

"No."

"Then what took you?"

"Nothing. Can I see the program?" She tilted it toward me, and I grabbed it and quickly opened it to the cast list.

Just then, Dirk stepped into the room and shook my hand. I raved about the show and introduced him to Natasha, whose only comment on the show was, "festive!" as she took back the program to use as a fan. "How did you wind up in this space?" I asked him.

"It used to be just a storage area. In exchange for my cleaning it out and making it into a theater space, they're letting me use it free all summer," he explained.

"I'm jealous. I used to write skits."

"Actually, we might be able to use some skits. Since we've got access to the space, we're doing a kind of revue night Wednesday nights."

"Cool!"

"Look, a bunch of us are getting together for a little cast party at my apartment on 14th Street. Why don't you come by?"

Natasha's eyes rolled upward in exasperation. "We'd love

to," I said.

On our way to 14th Street, Natasha and I avoided speaking. I found a deli on Second Avenue, where I bought a six pack. On our way toward the apartment, three different hooded figures with shadows for faces offered to sell me pot. "Smoke. Smoke. Smoke." I politely declined each time.

Natasha finally broke the silence: "Are you really going to write skits for that guy?"

"Hell, yes. I've always loved writing skits."

"Where are you going to find the time? You're already committed to editing the office newsletter."

"So, I'll back out."

"Back out? Do you realize how bad that makes you look? With the newsletter, you've got a real crack at attracting the attention of the upper management people."

"Is that what you think I want to do? Be some self-important office drone like–"I cut that sentence short, but not short enough.

"Then let me spell out the future for you. This is going to be a lot of fun at first, and probably a real ego trip. You might even convince yourself that it's going to take you someplace worthwhile, but gradually you'll discover it won't. Five years from now, you're going to wake up and realize you've wasted a significant part of your working adult life with these self-possessed low-life clowns."

We came to Dirk's street number. I buzzed Apartment H and waited for him to buzz me in the front door. Nothing happened. "Maybe you have the wrong address," Natasha offered.

As I went outside again to check the number, a rolled-up sock thudded against the sidewalk just a few feet away. I looked up to see an open window four flights up, and could just make out the dull roar of conversation.

Natasha gave me an incredulous look as I picked up the sock and unrolled it. Inside was a set of keys, one of which was labeled, "FD" and another of which said, "Apt."

We climbed the stairs to another world. I knocked, the door swung open, and Dirk embraced me and kissed me on the cheek. I looked down at his bare feet. The toenails of his left foot were painted red and he had wads of cotton between his toes. "Glad you could make it," he said, with laid back politeness. He also hugged Natasha. I handed him the keys he'd tossed down, rewrapped in the sock.

The room was full of semi-familiar faces from the cast. The tall Latino man who had played the general, was there. He still had the Spanish accent but was now wearing a flowery shirt and Chinos and acting a little swishy. Dirk directed me to the refrigerator, where I stashed the six pack sans two beers for Natasha and me. Then he returned to the couch by the window, and allowed the blonde beach bunny from the show to continue painting his toenails. "Is he gay?" Natasha whispered in my ear.

"I'm not sure what he is," I confessed.

In the middle of the room, the beautiful brunette actress was talking to the backstage redhead, the fat guy, and Jim, Dirk's mop-headed piano player. "There's the fat guy!" Natasha whispered, giggling.

"The fat guy has a name," I whispered back, censuring her. "Let me see the program."

She pulled it out of her purse. We looked at the listing for "Tourist" and saw his real name was "Pat Quinlan." Meanwhile, my gaze drifted down to "Beach Bunnies," which were played by Linda Powell and Angela Sardinia. Linda Powell sounded too blonde and WASP-y. I was betting that the beautiful brunette was Angela.

From his cozy corner of the couch, Dirk introduced us to this tall, skinny Jewish guy in glasses, "This is Rick. You remember him from the show, don't you?"

"Sure," I said automatically and then asked, "What part did

you play, exactly?"

"The rebel leader, actually," he explained, pouting and making yummy noises as he bit into a cracker with cheese. I had expected someone about twice his weight and, well, manly. He must have had a highly muscular torso underneath that sweater of his, but you just couldn't tell. I must have stared at him for a few seconds, and he said, "Really, I did. That was me."

"You did a great job, then," I said.

In the middle of it all was another guy I recognized from the Stanford crowd, with short brown hair, wearing black jeans, a black T-shirt, and glasses. It was Russell, who was a very clever writer, had co-edited a book with Sol Greenberg, and was now writing for *Spy, Vogue,* and *The Rolling Stone.* He had started to make a name for himself through personal exposes, slaughtering people messily in print, and I wondered whose life he was hammering away at this time.

Though he was drinking a beer, he wasn't really partying. He was busily typing something on a portable typewriter set up on a card table in the living room. The card table was not the best surface to be typing on, because every hunt-and-peck keystroke sounded like gunfire, and every time Russell pressed the carriage return, it sounded like a thunderclap and I thought it was going to tip the card table right over: *Clack! Clack! Clack! Shebang!*

Eventually, we sort of made our way over toward Jim, Pat, the redhead, and probably Angie group, ostensibly so Natasha could meet Pat, who was holding a magazine. As Natasha approached, he rolled the magazine up and cradled it in the crook of his arm. "I just wanted to say I thought you were the best part of the show!" Natasha said, shaking his hand.

"Why, thank you!" he said, with a dainty politeness unexpected in someone who weighed three hundred pounds and had a touch of Brooklyn in his voice. "Is there any part you especially savored, any morsel of my performance that you found especially delectable and delightful?"

"No, just the whole thing!" Natasha giggled.

"I'm glad you were able to make it!" the woman who was probably Angela said to me, playing hostess again.

"Yeah, you tracked Dirk right back to his lair!" the redhead piped in, and Natasha gave me a funny look. Then her eyes lit on the magazine.

"I was just showing my fellow cast members my first foray into fiction!" Pat explained to us, holding up the magazine.

"Oh, you write fiction? So does Rob, but he's never gotten anything published," Natasha volunteered, and when the rest of them looked at me, I smiled painfully and squinted at them. "Can I see it?"

"I fear it's not for the faint of heart, my dear," Pat said. Playfully, Natasha grabbed at it and looked at the front cover. It was a copy of *Gent*.

I had picked up a copy once or twice on the news stands. It was several steps below *Playboy* and *Penthouse* in terms of slickness, but not quite as crass, misogynist, and generally ugly as *Hustler*.

Natasha recognized it as a skin mag but probably didn't understand all these finer distinctions. Looking vaguely as if she had been slapped in the face, she just said, "You're probably right."

Clack. Clack. Clack. In the corner of the living room, Russell took a break from his hunting and pecking, took a swig of beer, and surveyed his own prose admiringly.

"My story is an interview with a dominatrix. But, since she was, alas, totally a figment of my imagination, I guess one could technically call it fiction," Pat confessed.

"Lemme see that," said the redhead, grabbing it out of his hand. "I was just saying to Angie I haven't had a chance to peruse this month's *Gent*." She leafed through it, opened the centerfold, and turned it ninety degrees. Then she showed it to Angela. My head drifted imperceptibly in the direction of the magazine.

"Does this look familiar? You're out raking leaves and then you bend over to look between your legs and that's when you realize that–oops,!–you forgot to put on any pants or underwear that morning," the redhead said. "God, it just happens to me all the time!"

Angela turned the page and chimed in, "Yeah, and then you think–what the hell–I'm out here naked in public anyway, I might as well masturbate with the rake handle." She turned another page. "Huh, you know, it never would have occurred to me to do that with a garden hose," she added, and then, flashing the page at Natasha, said, "Would it have occurred to you?"

Russell resumed his typing: *Clack. Clack. Clack. Clack. Clack. Shebang!*

Natasha said nothing but her eyes turned cold. "I hope they haven't offended you, my dear," Pat said to her, patting her gently on the back, gave the actresses a mock frown, and took back the magazine. "Ladies, please. I didn't bring my smut to the party just to have you ridicule it. This is my passion and my livelihood!"

"Look, we've got to go," Natasha said, rubbing her temples. "That typing is giving me a fucking headache." And so we did.

The next week, I began banging out three-minute skits on my Olympia portable typewriter and brought the first ones to Dirk's script meeting Wednesday night. Everyone loved them and the actors began rehearsing them. Thursday, I took out a membership at the West Side YMCA and began working out regularly, especially with the weights. Friday night, when we got together, Natasha told me she didn't want to see me any more. When I asked why, she said I had already dumped her–I just didn't know it yet.

THE VERDICT

For the first Chucklehead show, we were worried that the cast members would outnumber the audience, but miraculously, over 30 people showed up. And we pulled it off with minimal violence.

We had bandied a lot of names around, including National Insect Theatre, Laff-O-Rama, and Yucks For Bucks, but Chucklehead won out because nobody had a problem with it. Dirk's friend Paul, who videotaped all the shows Dirk put on, also manufactured postcards with a 1950s clip-art face. The amorphous cast, which included some of the cast of "Island Paradise," their friends, and their roommates, all mailed or handed out these postcards to their friends—that is, the ones who weren't already in the show. That's how we managed to put butts in over 30 folding chairs.

Tony, who had produced "Island Paradise," was also the producer of this show. He charged patrons $5 admission and also sold Piels beer in the lobby for a buck a cup. Selling beer not only helped offset the cost of renting the space, but also Dirk had long ago come to recognize that people would laugh at just about anything when they were drunk.

Dressed in jeans, a denim shirt, sunglasses, and a bandanna, with a camera hanging from my neck, I paced nervously backstage. I was already on my second Piels. I peered out at the 30+ audience members, sizing them up as a defense lawyer would size up a prospective jury. Many of the audience members were tall, young, thin, and beautiful men and women whom I assumed to be somebody's actor and actress friends. Would they be too vacuous to get our flaky material? There were also about half a dozen dowdy but earnest women of indeterminate age, whom I assumed to be fellow nurses that Pat's mother had invited. They didn't look as if they laughed more than once a year.

Sitting in the front row were two people I recognized, a man with curly red hair and glasses and a thin woman with short brunette hair and a toothy smile. They were writer friends of mine, Peter and Judy, who had worked with me on the ill-fated college textbook parody. Both were grinning with wide-eyed innocence. I was worried about how they would enjoy the show because neither of them was drinking.

I went over to them and meekly thanked them for coming. Looking at the program, full of Paul's weird clip-art, Peter asked, "What did you write?"

"I wrote the 'Baby Bottle' and the intro to 'Roach Razor,' but what I'm most proud of is 'The Nightmare Sketch,'" I explained.

They both nodded, smiling, but neither of them said anything. Finally, Peter chimed in, "We're really looking forward to it!"

Tony flicked the house lights off and on, signaling the beginning of the show. I bade farewell to my friends and ran backstage for the first skit. I poised a cigarette in my right hand.

For that skit, I had to be positioned at the top of a staircase, which just happened to be left over from "Island Paradise." The trouble was, it was dark backstage and I was virtually blind. I banged my shin against the first step, climbed onto it, and then fell down the other side of it. I resorted to scaling the stairs on my hands and knees before I thought of lowering my sunglasses for a moment. I reached the top of the staircase and stood there.

"Ladies and gentlemen, get ready to laugh till your eyes bleed!" Pat thundered over the backstage microphone. "For you are about to witness the most amazing and colossal spectacle ever witnessed on this continent or anywhere else! Put your hands together for Chuckleh-e-e-e-e-a-a-a-a-d!" This was greeted with polite, uncertain applause.

The Doors' "The End" faded in on the sound system and slowly peaked. Suddenly I was hit with a blinding light as Tony zapped me with the spotlight. The music faded back down again. With my cigarette-clad right hand, I stroked my beard, combed my hair back, and then began gesticulating wildly as I spoke. "Get ready, man! You're about to meet the man!" I raved, impersonating Dennis Hopper's character in "Apocalypse Now." Some people tittered because they immediately picked up on the allusion. Others tittered because they were just along for the ride. "He's who this whole thing is about! Me—I'm just a small man! He's a very big man. He walks around quoting T. S. Elliot—I'd rather be a pair of ragged claws—He knows things! And now he's about to speak!"

The spotlight went down, thus ending my debut performance.

Lights up on Pat, dressed in a bathrobe and bald wig and holding a large bowl of water, impersonating Marlon Brando's Kurtz. Languidly, he scooped up a handful of water from the bowl and let it trickle over the crown of his bald head. "The horror! The horror! I'm haunted by . . . the image of a . . . cockroach . . . crawling along the edge . . . of a razor blade . . . "

The whole skit turned out to be an advertisement for a product called Roach Razor ("Terminate those roaches—with extreme prejudice!"). As the lights went down, the audience laughed and applauded.

Moments later, Jim played "Twinkle, Twinkle Little Star" on his Casio. Rose, dressed in pajamas and pigtails and carrying a Teddy bear by its left leg, peeked sheepishly out from behind the curtain. For several seconds, she played peek-a-boo with the audience. Then, amidst titters, she came out, introduced herself as Susie, and delivered a string of the raunchiest jokes I'd ever heard with this gleefully bratty look on her face. Suddenly, I wasn't sure whether Rose was pretending to be Susie on stage or whether Susie was pretending to be Rose in everyday life.

Susie established an easy rapport with the audience, asking them pointed questions an adult could never get away with, like: "Are you two together or what?"

At one point, a woman in the audience said, "Aren't you up past your bedtime, little girl?"

"Nyyyooo," Susie answered defiantly. "How late does your mother let you stay up?"

"I don't have a mother because she died of cancer!" the woman called back bitterly. Oh my God!

The audience was dead silent, waiting to see how Rose/Susie was going to respond. Rose's–or maybe Susie's–eyes glazed over for maybe half a second, and then a devilish glee came over Susie's face. "Then you can stay up as late as you want!"

The audience roared. It was a brilliant comeback. I felt a little sorry for the woman whose mother died of cancer, but she shouldn't have been heckling Rose.

The audience continued laughing and applauding throughout "The Baby Bottle," a really weird skit I wrote about an explorer grandfather (Pat) giving a nervous and uncomfortable middle-class whitebread family (Dirk, Rose, and a new actor named Spanky) a curiosity from his travels–an embryo in a bottle. They laughed and applauded through Pat's "Hot Seat," a game show parody in which contestants (Angie and Pat) vie for the privilege of throwing the switch on a death row convict (me) strapped into an electric chair. They managed to laugh and applaud through another 10 quirky sketches, which were separated by two minutes of noisy furniture moving and Casio playing by Tim, but the claps duller and less frequent.

And then it was time for my beloved "Nightmare Sketch." I was sick to my stomach with stage fright, even though it was my skit–not me–that was about to go on stage. Dirk, standing backstage, looked at his watch, and I could sense something was amiss.

"The show is really going a lot longer than I had expected, and the audience is starting to fade on us," he whispered nervously. "We're going to have to skip 'The Nightmare Sketch.'"

Even though he had the choice role of Eliot, he had never liked the skit. When we read it at the script meeting, everyone had laughed enthusiastically, but Dirk argued that the skit was mean-spirited, crass, sophomoric, and just plain weird. The cast countered that it was just plain funny. Dirk made sure it had the lowest priority at the rehearsals, but the cast always reminded him to run through it.

I think what ultimately kept the skit on track was the fact that Angie was in it. Jim was Dirk's best friend and the show's musical director, and so he was indispensable. Angie was Jim's girlfriend, and she often complained that she didn't have any fun roles in the show—except for Deirdre in "The Nightmare Sketch." If Dirk had killed the skit, Angie would have made Jim's life miserable, and in turn Jim would have made Dirk's life miserable.

But now, Dirk was making a last-ditch effort to bury the sucker before it ever reached the stage.

If I hadn't had three and a half beers over the course of the show, I wouldn't have done what I did next. I grabbed Dirk, about six inches taller than me, and slammed him against the wall of the proscenium. Then I continued to slam him against the wall for punctuation. "So help me God, you're not killing my script!" *Slam.* "Do the skit, you sonofabitch!" *Slam.* "Do the script or I'll fucking kill you!" *Slam.*

He launched me backward about five feet, turned, and walked away. Then he proceeded to do the skit and do it beautifully. When the lights came up on stage, he showed not the slightest hint of having been assaulted backstage. He and Angie had this wonderful telepathic chemistry together as they carried out their mean and perverted acts on Roger, played by Pat.

The audience didn't just laugh. Some of them guffawed.

ROB DINSMOOR

Some brayed like donkeys. One of the nurses sounded as if she were choking on her own tongue. Every laugh coursed through my veins like a snort of cocaine, made even more delicious by the sweet, numbing taste of revenge. "Yeah! Yeah! How do you like that, you fucker?" I whispered at Dirk, pounding my fist into the air. As the skit climaxed and ended, the applause sounded like a fireworks finale on the Fourth of July. Sweet Jesus, I had never felt a rush like that!

"Ladies and gentlemen, your eyes don't deceive you! You have just witnessed Chucklehead!" Pat thundered over the backstage mike, and then proceeded to name every performer, as we all took a curtain call. The audience continued to clap enthusiastically through most of it. "Thank you for coming and goodnight!"

The stage lights dimmed and the house lights went up. The performers all went out to meet their public, and I could hear everyone congratulating everybody else. Pat was soaking up the attention from all of the nurses, who no longer looked dowdy, but energized and dazzled.

The woman in the audience who had made the cancer crack spotted Rose, who was talking with a group of beautiful people, and made a beeline for her. When she reached her, she spun Rose around and looked her in the eye. "Arlene!" Rose said, hugging her. "Thanks a lot for the cancer line. Why do you blurt out shit like that during my monologues?"

"Keeps you on your toes, darling. I think you handled it beautifully."

Peter and Judy came up to me, smiling. "That was great!" Peter said, patting me on the back. "Is there any chance of Judy and I getting in on the fun?"

"Absolutely!" I said. "We need more writers–good writers!"

Dirk, who was acquainted with Peter and Judy, came over to shake their hands and thank them for coming. "We loved you in 'The Nightmare Sketch,'" Peter said. I gloated at Dirk once again, but he wasn't making any eye contact.

"Thanks—but I can't take all the credit. It was a great script," Dirk said.

"Thanks . . ." I muttered, but Dirk at least pretended not to hear as he floated over to the next familiar face.

I shook hands with everyone and took particular delight in hugging Angie, who was still wearing a tight, short skirt from "The Nightmare Sketch." "You were great—especially in Nightmare!" I said.

"Thanks for giving me a good part!" she purred in my ear. She inserted her polished, manicured red fingernails into the pocket of my shirt and fished a cigarette out of my pack. Then she reached into my front pants pocket, withdrew my lighter, lit her cigarette, and tucked it back in. "Write me some more!" she said, exhaling smoke, turned, and walked away.

In the back corner of the house, Paul was disconnecting his video equipment and placing it carefully into its perfectly fitted padded bags. "How'd it look?"

"Good," he said. "Congratulations on 'The Nightmare Sketch.' I think it went over well."

"Thanks! Can I get a copy of that sometime?"

"Yeah. I'll make copies of the show for everyone. I'll have to edit out the breaks between the skits, though. They last forever. Dirk's going to have to find a way to fill that time."

Backstage, I packed all my crap into a duffle bag and slung it over my shoulder in preparation for the long, late subway ride out to Sheepshead Bay in Brooklyn. As I came out into the lobby, where Dirk was putting the last of the empty Piels bottles in a box for recycling. As I walked by, I sneaked a glance at him as he was sneaking a glance at me and we could no longer pretend to ignore each other. "I'm sorry I almost killed your script, man," he said, and suddenly my eyes started to tear up.

"I'm sorry, I, uh, slammed you against the wall. Repeatedly.

And threatened to kill you," I said, my voice now starting to crack.

Before I knew it, Dirk's hands were coming at me. He grabbed me by the shoulders and slammed me forcefully against his own chest in a power hug. "That's all right, man. I still love you."

THE NIGHTMARE SKETCH

CHARACTERS
ROGER (PAT)
ELLIOT (DIRK)
DIERDRE (ANGIE)

ROGER is sitting in a chair with rollers, watching TV. He is a pig. ELLIOT and DIERDRE are sitting on a nearby couch, looking restless.

ELLIOT
Say, uh, Roger. There's a Don Rickles film festival at the Waverly. Maybe if you run, you can still catch it.

ROGER
Naw, I think I'll stay here and watch "Teenage Sex Zombies."

ELLIOT
But Roger. You've been staying with us for two weeks now. Dierdre and I would kind of like to be alone for the night.

ROGER
You two go ahead and do what you want. I'll be wrapped up in the movie.

ROGER starts to nod off a little.

DEIRDRE
(feigning a yawn)
Say, you look like you're fading on us, Roger.

ELLIOT
Roger, are you . . . asleep?

ELLIOT snaps his finger in front of ROGER. ROGER doesn't respond.

He's asleep! Let's do it! How about something with the Titanic?

DIERDRE
That one's been done to death.

ROGER
(murmuring in his sleep)
Oh. . . Ginger . . . Ginger . . .

DIERDRE
Who's Ginger?

ELLIOT
Some girl he met in Alabama. I've got an idea. Say, who's that over there, Roger? I can't make out her face.

ROGER
Wha–?

ELLIOT
Why, it's Ginger!

ROGER
Ginger—oh, hi, Ginger!

DIERDRE
(snuggling up to him, in a Southern accent)
Oh, Roger Roger Roger! I think it's a wonderful thing you're doing.
Going off with the boys in blue to fight for democracy in Viet Nam!

ELLIOT
(shaking his hand, in an authoritative voice)
Hell of a thing you're doing, Roger. Hold on. The plane's taking off.

ELLIOT pushes the chair forward.

DIERDRE
(her voice fading)
Bye, Roger! Bye . . .

ELLIOT
No time for boot camp, Roger. It's straight to Me Lai!

ROGER looks very, very upset. He is not dreaming good dreams.
ELLIOT and DIERDRE ride him around in the chair a bit.
ELLIOT grabs a basket of props, from which he pulls a tiny house-
plant. He tickles Roger's face with the plant.

Pretty horrible jungle—eh, Roger? I haven't spotted any Viet Cong
yet, but the place is literally crawling with spiders. Big ones, too.

ELLIOT and DIERDRE crawl all over ROGER with their hands.
ELLIOT whacks his own hand.

ELLIOT
Got it. Uh oh. It was a female. I hope it didn't lay any eggs in your underpants.

ROGER grimaces.

Who's that coming over the hill, Roger? I can't make out their faces.

ROGER
I don't . . . can't see . . .

DIERDRE begins muttering something that sounds vaguely like Vietnamese.

ELLIOT
Women and children from the village, Roger! They're bringing us baskets of fruit to thank us for saving their village.

ROGER smiles.

My God! Those aren't fruit! Those are live hand grenades! It's a suicide squad! Grab your machine gun! Kill the slopes!

ELLIOT takes an umbrella from his prop basket and puts it in Roger's hand, rattling it back and forth and making machine-gun sounds.

ELLIOT
My God! Those weren't hand grenades! Those were baskets of fruit after all! You're a murderer, Roger!

ELLIOT & DIERDRE
(in unison)
Murderer! Murderer! Murderer!

ROGER starts wimpering.

DIERDRE
Roger–it's me, Ginger! You were just having a bad dream, honey!
You're not in Viet Nam! You're back with me in Mobile, Alabama!

ROGER smiles, relieved.

And I've got some wonderful news! I'm gonna have a baby!

ELLIOT
Congratulations, Roger! Imagine–you're a father! A baby!

ELLIOT & DIERDRE
(in unison)
A baby! A baby! A baby!

ROGER is far from pleased. He mutters confused protests.

ELLIOT
(authoritatively)
Having a baby is an awesome responsibility, Roger. Looks like
you'll have to quit law school and become a file clerk.

DIERDRE
(excitedly)
We'll move into a trailer park and live there the rest of our lives–
just you, me, and the baby!

DIERDRE mimics a baby crying.

ELLIOT
Congratulations, Roger! Your wife just gave birth to quintuplets—all joined together at the spine!

ELLIOT & DIERDRE
(in unison)
The spine! The spine! The spine!

ROGER is visibly upset.

ELLIOT
These days, Siamese quintuplets can lead relatively normal lives. Look over there. Your wife's nursing them!

ELLIOT and DIERDRE make horrible suckling sounds and ROGER starts crying. DIERDRE jostles ROGER to the edge of consciousness.

DIERDRE
Wake up, Roger. The ride's beginning!

ELLIOT begins tilting the chair back.

Imagine, the tallest roller coaster in the world, and we're the first ones to ride it! Up, up, up we go to the top of Dead Man's peak! Imagine—we're over 300 feet off the ground! Look—there's the park manager, waving to us. What's he saying?

ELLIOT
(in a faraway voice)
Get off, you fools! The ride's not ready!

DIERDRE
Down we go!

ELLIOT tilts the chair forward, sending ROGER screaming to the floor. Quickly, they return to the couch as he wakes up.

ELLIOT
Is something the matter, Roger?

ROGER
I just had the most horrible nightmare of my life–something about roller coasters joined together at the spine. I'm going out for some fresh air. See you later.

DIERDRE
(in Southern accent)
Bye bye!

ROGER cringes and exits. ELLIOT and DIERDRE laugh.

DIERDRE
That was great!

ELLIOT
That was even better than the Titanic.

DIERDRE
So what do you want to do now?

ELLIOT turns to DIERDRE and starts to kiss her. He changes his mind and turns away.

ELLIOT
When do you suppose Roger's coming back?

DIERDRE
I don't know. Hope it's soon.

BLACKOUT.

THE SHOOT

Gill, the owner of The Dive ("a sleazy bar for nice people"), unlocked and raised the gate, unlocked the front door, and turned on the lights for us one Saturday morning. "I'll be back around noon to lock up again," he said, retreating past the closed, gated Indian import stores that lined West 29th Street. "Try not to make a mess."

We early arrivals surveyed the room. The floor, walls, and ceiling were black or some color indistinguishable from it. Wobbly chairs were piled in one corner, and small, black tables, which seemed to be made of kindling, were stacked on top of each other. The place was filthy, our soles stuck to the floor, and the room stank of stale beer and cigarettes. The lock and doorknob of the one tiny unisex bathroom were broken. On the wall beside the bathroom was a message crudely carved into the wall: "Employees wash hands," which was Gill's idea of a joke, since someone had ripped the pipes out of the sink months earlier.

The Dive was exactly the way it had always been right before our shows, and actually Gill liked it like that.

That morning, we were there to shoot one of our video segments. The setting was supposed to be an upscale yuppie bar. We had a lot of work ahead of us.

Our crew worked telepathically, like individual neurons in some giant, disembodied brain. Paul, our video czar, assembled all of his equipment in a corner: Camera, tape deck, portable color TV, microphones, lights, batteries, and every conceivable type of cable and adapter. It was good stuff, generously on loan to us from his company without their knowledge or consent.

Our troupe, Chucklehead, had started out just performing live skits, but the one- to two-minute blackouts between them had become very awkward. Meanwhile, with Paul's video wizardry, we were creating a backlog of videos that could be plugged in between the skits. In fact, we had so much more control over the videos, especially their timing, that they were generally funnier than the skits. Furthermore, if they worked once, they generally always worked, and gradually they became part of our trademark.

The script was one of mine called "Mort's Date." It was a sequel to another successful video called "Mort's Break-Up." Shot from the point of view of a silent and emotionally paralyzed character named Mort, "Mort's Break-Up" starts with Mort eating a bowl of cereal in Jim and Angie's tiny apartment in the West Village. The camera looks up to see Mort's girlfriend, played by Rose, delivering a scalding harangue about Mort being out of work and just hanging around the apartment all day, scraping calluses off his feet. He doesn't respond the entire time she delivers this monologue, but after she walks out the door, he says, "Don't go!" "Mort's Break-Up" had been one of the key videos for the last several shows, my own personal pride and joy, but now it was starting to get old.

I began to unstack the tables and chairs and arrange them to look vaguely like what I thought tables and chairs in a respectable establishment might look like. Soon Angie stepped in the door with her hallmark garbage bag full of costumes, followed by a short, stocky, sort of simpering character I assumed to be one of the strays that always followed her home from acting classes. From her bag, she pulled some sort of old teal dress, which she threw over one of the tables, and a roll of duct tape, from which she bit and tore long strips she used to affix the ends of the dress under the tabletop. Finally, she pulled out some nice candle she had undoubtedly lifted from one of the restaurants where she waitressed, and began putting them on the Dive's tables. Paul had already mounted the camera on a tripod and hooked it up, and on the portable monitor, the table looked pretty damn impressive

By selectively lighting the Dive, Paul was able to establish that it was a bar without really showing how squalid it was. In fact, on the TV, the Dive looked quite cozy and discreet. Gill himself would never have recognized it.

Angie held up three different outfits from her garbage bag. "Which one would Lori be wearing?" Naturally, I pointed to the one with the shortest skirt, not just because I liked Angie in shorter skirts but because the character of Lori was based on a beautiful Jewish blabbermouth I had known who wore short skirts.

About half a minute later, she tapped me on the shoulder. When I turned around, she was wearing it. "What do you think?"

I thought I should have been paying better attention. "Looks great!" I said.

Dirk showed up with his girlfriend Alicia, another California transplant from Stanford, and Tony, our sleazy, untalented, self-described "producer" who did very little but hang around and wait for us to become famous. Dirk parked Alicia on a barstool and immediately went to work with Paul. As our artistic director, Dirk generally liked to be in charge, but he was completely helpless around video equipment and had to concede to Paul, who was a video wizard. Tony, stroking his mustache, contented himself asking Paul all sorts of pointless technical questions, like whether he was using zirconium lights and whether the camera was equipped with Dolby sound. Paul patiently answered his questions at first, but eventually at least pretended to be distracted by the job at hand.

Paul was the master of the cheap special effect, often opting for effects and solutions that were ridiculously simple. A year ago, he had shot a segment in which Dirk and I, rolling on the ground and shrieking horribly, are attacked by a crazed mountaineer's vengeful hawk pet. Everyone watching it wondered how Paul was able to get the cheesy hawk puppet—a crude assemblage of socks, felt, and pipe cleaners–to actually fly through the air and attack us. Was the hawk on a string of some sort? Was it actually one of those remote-control toy airplanes camouflaged as a hawk? Did Paul use a matte shot? Was some sort of stop-action animation involved? The simple truth was that, most of the time, the right wing of the hawk was attached to a long stick. If you were cognizant of this fact when you watched the video, you would notice that the hawk's right wing was often at the very edge of the frame. If you didn't know this, the hawk simply flew. The end result was devastatingly funny.

At Paul's request, Angie took her seat at the table so he could check the lighting and mis en scene. Dirk pointed to Angie's chubby friend and asked, "Hey, what's your name?"

"Phil–"

"–yeah, Phil. You want to be the bartender?"

"Sure!" said Phil, and moved behind the bar. "Do I have any lines?"

"Not right now but you will," Dirk said, trying to shut him up. At this point, he didn't need an actor, just a body.

Within 20 minutes, everybody knew their lines, everyone was in position, and we were ready to shoot. Just as in Hitchcock's flawed masterpiece, "Rope," we were going to do this whole thing in a single take. That meant there was no fixing things later–if anyone fucked up, we had to start all over again.

As in the first video, Paul shot from Mort's POV, while I held a directional mike tied to a big stick just outside the frame. Dirk served as Mort's hands. As Paul shot over Dirk's shoulder, weaving ever so slightly left and right, Phil handed Dirk a glass of beer and intoned "Here you go. From now on, order coffee?" Alicia, still seated at the bar, brushed back her teased sun-bleached hair and gave the camera the most snobby, sneering, disgusted look I have ever seen. It was a little disturbing how easily that expression came to her.

"Cut!" Dirk said, and then took a little sidebar with Phil. "Listen, that line about the coffee. It's not a question, it's an order. You're not asking him whether he's ordering coffee. You're telling him to. You're cutting him off because he's already drunk. Got it?"

"Sure."

Everyone took their places again. In total unison, Dirk and Paul weaved up to the bar. "Here you go," said Phil. "From now on, order coffee?"

"Cut!" Dirk snapped, and now his laid-back surfer-dude persona was starting to fade away like a tan in September. He combed his hand back through his sandy hair and said, "Yeah, man. Remember, it's an order—not a question. From now on . . ."

"From now on . . ." Phil repeated.

". . . order coffee."

". . . order coffee."

"Perfect, man. You're a pro."

We ran it again. And again. And again. Each time, Phil found a new way of saying the line that just wasn't right, despite Dirk's repeated coaching. "Here you go. From *now on*, order coffee?" "From now on, *order* coffee." "Here, you go order coffee now."

Everyone except for Phil was getting more and more tired and anxious as the taping proceeded. Finally, during one take, while Phil was posing his line in the form of a question, Dirk inexplicably didn't yell "Cut!" The scene moved forward, and everyone was caught off guard. It gave a strange intensity to their acting.

With Paul shooting over his shoulder, Dirk clumsily carried the beer over to the table, while I sidled alongside with a microphone on a stick. On the table, there were already eight empty glasses and an ashtray full of butts. Dirk sat down, raised the trembling glass up to a point just below the camera lens, and sighed.

That was the last take we needed to do. From Phil's pleading with the camera to order coffee to the Angie's nervous, hyper performance, the final product was pure gold. Lori (Angie) sits down opposite the viewer and says, "Hi, Mort! It looks like you started without me!" From that point on, she talks expansively about herself in a long, hilarious monologue while Mort continues to hoist beers to his lips. Finally, some sleazy, mustached young Lothario (our producer Tony) taps her on the shoulder and says, "Didn't we have a share together on Fire Island?" winks condescendingly at the camera, and steals Lori away under the guise of going to look at pictures from Fire Island. It was the only time Tony ever acted in the troupe, and he was extremely convincing. The take ended with Dirk and Paul stumbling over a chair together, and then a fade out as Mort loses consciousness.

After we finished that take, Dirk insisted that Paul rewind it for him. Dirk put on the headphones and viewed the playback through the camera's viewfinder. His shrill laughter intimated that it was a keeper. It was to become one of the show's staples for the next year and a half. I couldn't help but think how much different the video might have turned out had Phil not flubbed his line half a dozen times in a row.

After the shoot was done and we were gathering up our stuff, Dirk extended his hand to Phil. "Hey, thanks a lot, man. Are you coming to the show?"

"What show?" Phil asked.

"The next Chucklehead performance! Didn't Angie tell you what this shoot was about?"

"Who's Angie?"

Dirk pointed. "That beautiful Mediterranean babe over there, dude. I thought you came in with her!"

"No. I just saw people gathering in here and decided to come in and check it out."

Still trying to assimilate all this newfound knowledge, Dirk said, "Well, we're playing here Fridays and Saturdays starting at the end of this month. So, come on by, man. We'll put you on the comp list!"

"Thanks, I'll be there!" said Phil, smiling in wonderment as he strolled out the door.

We never saw him again.

ROB DINSMOOR

NOTHING SPECIAL

I am not by nature a clock watcher, but after 3 p.m., I constantly looked up from my galley proofs to see if the minute hand had suddenly leapt forward. It never had. Finally, when the hour hand was on the five and I judged that the minute hand was in the dead center of twelve, I picked up the phone and called Angie. She had said she would be back by five, and we could make dinner plans then.

As soon as she picked up the phone, she said, "Hi, Rob! Aren't you curious about how I knew it was you?"

"Who else would be anal enough to call you at exactly five o'clock–at exactly the time we'd agreed on?"

She laughed. "Hey, you know what you're like! I like people who know what they're like!"

And so we went out for sushi that evening. When I arrived, she was already seated at the sushi bar. She was just finishing up the Sunday New York Times crossword puzzle–in pen–and she put it in her purse. The fact that she had finished it fazed me a little, but I let it go.

As we dined in the briny, intoxicating air of the sushi bar, she told me about her auditions and her call-backs. I told her about mailing a synopsis of my one-act play around to theatres. "Why?" she asked.

"Because I want to get it produced!"

"Why are you mailing it? Do you want it to wind up in the trash?"

"You have a better idea?"

"You should take it around to the theatres. Demand that

they look at it. If they don't want to look at it, ask them why not. Then, if they take it and agree to read it, call them back and ask them if they've read it. If they haven't, ask why not."

"That's not my style. I let the work speak for itself," I said, picking tiny pieces of flying fish roe off of one of my sushi rolls.

"Your play can't talk. You can. Spanky's friend Dave always peddles his plays in person. And you know his friend Ron? He's always pulling weird shit to get his head shot around. One time he dressed up like a pizza delivery guy and delivered a pizza to a talent agency. No one owned up to ordering the pizza, so he just left it in the reception area and said it was on the house. Right underneath the pizza, in a big plastic bag, were half a dozen of his head shots with the resume on the back."

I watched the sushi chef, a large, intimidatingly gleeful Japanese man wearing glasses, sharpen his knife, toss an apple in the air, and impale it dead-center on his blade. With one quick motion, he deftly cut a spiral into its flesh and twisted it into an elaborate conical garnish. "Well, did he get representation that way?" I finally asked.

"I don't know."

"Then, what's the point? I'm not going to pull that kind of crap. Maybe the trouble is he has no talent," I said.

"And you think you do?"

The comment hit me like a slap in the face. "Yeah."

"Look, there are eight million people living in Manhattan, and a huge percentage of them are looking to make it big in acting or writing."

"I live in Brooklyn–"

"If we include the five boroughs, we're talking more like fifteen to sixteen million people, I think, but let's give you the benefit of the doubt. Among the millions of people in the city who want to make it big writing, what makes you so special?"

"I'm smart and I'm funny and I've got a track record. I was

editor of my college humor magazine. I won two prizes in college for writing comedy plays."

"Okay, so you made a name for yourself in college–"

"–Ivy League college–" I corrected, jabbing a chopstick at her.

"Maybe that narrows the field to a few thousand people. What else have you got?"

"I'm a science writer, and I'm from the Midwest. Both of those things give me sort of a unique perspective." I watched the sushi chef roll a long, pink cylinder of raw tuna in rice and seaweed.

"Okay, so maybe one-tenth of the people who come here to write are from the Midwest. Maybe one-fifth of the people who come here to write wind up as science writers. Given all this, there are still hundreds of people in the city who, on paper, look exactly like you do, have backgrounds and stories identical to yours, and they're all applying for exactly the same gigs you are. If some agent or producer or editor or whoever passes on you and your unique talent, there are hundreds of other science-writing Midwesterners identical to you lining up to take your place. You're nothing special."

I gaped at her unable to believe she was saying something so horrible about me. It filled me with misery because I did not want to live in a world in which I wasn't a celebrated writer. "Look, I'm not trying to insult you. All I'm trying to point out is that you've got to have an edge–to have the pure force of will to do something the other five hundred prize-winningly funny Ivy-League science-writing Midwest shmoes would be unwilling to do."

Having finished her monologue, she took a long gulp of beer and looked vacantly at the wall. God she's beautiful, I thought. Beneath her aqualine nose, her lips were dark and sensuous–but the things that came out of them! I winced as the sushi chef, with diabolical force and precision, hacked the cylinder of tuna into six identical tuna rolls.

I took a deep breath, turned to Angie with cadaver eyes, and said in a slow, calm, icy monotone: "Well, what do you know, really? You're just an ordinary little girl living in an ordinary little town. You wake up every morning of your life and you know perfectly well there's nothing in the world to trouble you. You go through your ordinary little day and at night you sleep your untroubled, ordinary little sleep filled with peaceful, stupid dreams."

Suddenly, for the first time that evening, Angie was staring directly into my eyes, lips slightly parted.

"How do you know what the world is like?" I continued. "Do you know that the world is a foul sty? Do you if you ripped the fronts off all the houses, you'd find swine? The world's a hell! What does it matter what anybody does or what happens in it?" Angie's eyes were now dilated, her mouth gaped, and her breathing was rapid and shallow. That's when I could no longer contain myself and broke down laughing.

"Jesus Christ! What the hell was that?"

"Joseph Cotton's speech to his favorite niece in 'Shadow of a Doubt.' He's a serial killer known as the 'Merry Widow Strangler.' It was Hitchcock's favorite one of his films—mine too—and that's my favorite monologue, so I memorized it."

She actually shivered. For a moment, I thought I'd totally alienated her. "Wow! Can you write that down for me sometime?"

Smiling opaquely, the sushi chef came over to our table, presented us with an offering—a small plate of tuna shavings garnished with ginger, wasabe, and seaweed—and gave me a subtle bow.

SHAMELESS ON SECOND AVENUE

A ll this bother for five seconds of footage.

It was Saturday morning and our HQ for this particular shoot was Russell's apartment on Second Avenue, near 12th Street. Everything was ready to go except the star of the segment. "It's now or never, Rob," Jim said, and suddenly he, Paul, Russell, Dirk, Rose, and Angie were all staring at me expectantly. I pulled off my polo shirt, then undid my belt, dropped my jeans, and took them off.

Now I was wearing nothing but navy blue bikini briefs. Angie came up to me with a blue towel. "Here's your cape, honey," she said, draping it over my back and safety-pinning the ends together under my chin.

"Can I get a bathrobe or something?" I pleaded. "I'm not going out without a bathrobe."

On cue, Russell tossed me a bathrobe from his bedroom. I caught it in one hand and put it on. The sleeves were several inches too long for me, but it would have to do. Enough stalling. On with the show.

"Why was I chosen for this?" I had asked, when the video script was first read.

"Your regal bearing and your beard," Dirk had explained.

En masse, we descended the staircase of Russell's apartment building. Paul, Dirk, Russell, and Rose all carried pieces of video equipment. Angie carried my crown and scepter. Jim carried a couple of very ripe tomatoes.

It was a sunny summer Saturday morning, and Second Avenue was teeming with activity: Old Russian Jews on their way to the deli, punks on their way to SoHo or Alphabet City, young urban professional couples pushing strollers, younger single professionals riding bikes on the street or roller skates on the sidewalk.

And, of course, a guy in a bathrobe and a video crew gathering at the corner.

Paul set up shop on the edge of the sidewalk next to a wrought-iron fence. He put down the tripod, carefully pulling down its legs to the right height, set up the camera, plugged it into his deck, and checked the battery. He pulled the camera back a few steps and adjusted the zoom to make sure that I was centered and just enough of the street and the wrought-iron fence were in the frame. Never one to trust any of the camera's automatic settings, he adjusted the focus, adjusted the light, and adjusted the focus again. It was all taking so long.

The segment was a fake ad for a fake magazine called "Paranoia Today," a take-off on paranoid tabloids. Segments included, "AIDS: The Toilet Seat Connection" and "People Are Talking About . . . YOU." My segment was part of the intro: "Do you ever get the feeling people are making fun of you?" It featured the emperor with no clothes, walking down Second Avenue, with people laughing at him.

Paul was ready. Dirk, Russell, Rose, and Angie were all set to walk by from the opposite direction, point and laugh. Jim was poised with the tomatoes. Paul pointed to me. "All right, Rob. We're ready for you."

I took off the bathrobe and hung it on the wrought iron fence behind the camera. I put on my crown and picked up my scepter. Then I walked about thirty feet down the sidewalk, away from the camera.

Everything was okay. I had worked out. I had lost my spare tire and my love handles months ago. I was no Arnold Schwarzenegger, but I had a slim, muscular body. I glanced down briefly at the slightly bulging navy blue parcel beneath my waist and found myself wondering exactly what constituted indecent exposure under the law. As people walked to and fro, I avoided making eye contact with them. I kept a confident smile ironed onto my face, even though my pulse was racing and my cheeks were beginning to flush.

Then I noticed something: No one was looking at me!

This was, after all, New York City. How many times had I walked down the street, seeing people wearing outlandish clothing? How many leather queens? How many women in tight vinyl pants? How many half-naked homeless people in rags, pissing or taking a dump on the sidewalk in full view of everyone? How many hookers with hot pants wedged way up their butts? How many punks with shaved heads or green or orange Mohawks? Why would anyone pay the slightest attention to a guy in bikini briefs wearing a towel cape and a cardboard crown and carrying a scepter?

As strangers passed by, I now stared right at them, but they never even glanced in my direction. I smiled warmly at a middle-aged woman walking some sort of lap dog down the street. I stooped and patted the dog until the woman, looking off in the distance with a slight smirk, managed to pull the dog forward again. I was invisible!

It reminded me of my all-time favorite dream. It started out as a typical anxiety-ridden dream in which I'm standing in line, totally naked, to be seated at a very fancy restaurant. Suddenly, I realize how ridiculous the situation is, that I'm actually dreaming, that it's my dream, and that it is completely under my control. The maitre d' comes along and leads me to my seat. I put my naked butt right down on that fancy chair and discreetly cross my legs. He hands me the menu and asks me if there's anything I'd like, and I order a glass of Merlot. All the while, I'm snickering to myself, because neither he nor the other snooty patrons of this snooty restaurant realize that I am totally bare-ass, buck naked.

Remembering that dream, I once again felt that euphoric sense of power. I was invisible. I was invincible!

"Action!" Paul called. Shielded by my new-found aura, I marched confidently down Second Avenue toward the camera in my blue bikini briefs, never so proud in my life. Russell, Dirk, Rose, and Angie all passed by on cue, pointed, and laughed at me. And it was okay, because they were all my friends. They just wanted my scene to work. It was a glorious moment! I was king of the world!

Something struck me in the face hard enough to jolt my head back, then make my ears ring and my cheeks tingle. Jim stood laughing, behind the camera, about six feet away. He was supposed to lob the tomato gently into my face. Instead, he had launched it right into my face with all his might at point-blank range. Tomato juice dripping down my chin, I looked at him with shock and betrayal. "Cut!" Paul called out and everybody laughed.

"You sonofabitch!" I yelled at Jim.

"You should see the look on your face!" he responded, still laughing.

Angie patted my face clean with my cape, draped the bathrobe over my back, and gave me a gentle pat. Dirk was saying to Paul, "Quick. Rewind. Lemme see it!"

Paul rewound and Dirk looked through the viewfinder. Suddenly Dirk burst out laughing so hard he doubled over and held his stomach. Then Russell wanted to see it. Everyone wanted to see it. When I finally got to see it, I could appreciate the beauty of that shot. The king walking down the street, oh so confident, even though everyone is laughing at him. Then the tomatoes hit and he has this look of total bewilderment and, at that exact moment, realizes that he's a laughingstock. It was a keeper.

We all walked back to Russell's apartment, having captured an excellent piece of footage. I had mixed feelings. I had just given the troupe a wonderful and heart-felt performance, but had done so at the expense of my self-respect.

Suddenly, I turned to Angie and asked, "Hey, if you were some babe sitting in the audience and you saw that footage, would you want to do me?"

"Absolutely," she said. "You know, during the shoot, Rose turned to me and said, 'That Rob has such a cute little body.'"

And life was good again.

COUNT YOUR FRIENDS
AFTER THE SHOW

Count your friends *after* the show," Spanky always said. It was like his mantra. It became a saying of mine, too, after one show in May of 1986.

I was sitting in the audience at the Judith Anderson Theatre, waiting for the show to begin, drinking beer out of a bottle in a brown paper bag. Russell was doing the videos for that gig, and a lighting guy came with the theater, so I had no particular role in that show. In fact, I had practically nothing to do with that show at all. I had only one skit in the show, and it wasn't even one I liked.

I was burnt out. In the first two years, I had banged out 20 scripts that got shot or performed, and another 60 that didn't. Chucklehead audiences had a lot of repeat offenders, and even tried and true material became old really, really fast and had to be replaced. We had four writers churning out scripts, and now most of the actors felt compelled to try their hand at writing, and you had to let at least a few of their scripts through because you couldn't afford to alienate them. Sometimes you hoped someone else would dump on them because you didn't want to be the one.

There was constant pressure to produce, produce, produce. Crank 'em out fast. Bring at least three or four of 'em to a meeting. Maybe the group will like one. Maybe one of the ones the group likes will actually get done. That is, if Russell and Dirk don't get at it.

During script meetings, Russell braced himself in the chair and waited. He was a skit shooter. As soon as someone else's script became airborne and threatened to soar, Russell would point both barrels of his glasses at it, cock his eyelids together, and blam! "I've got a real problem with it."

While he described what was wrong with the script, why the ending seemed tagged on, why it didn't make sense, why it was unimaginative and formulaic, why it was just plain stupid and would be embarrassing to put on stage, he would massage his temples and his forehead and sometimes rub his eyes back into their sockets.

His body language was clear: He was a fair and reasonable guy and it really, really pained him to have to pick apart other people's scripts. Hell, it pained him just to have to listen to them in the first place!

Dirk's assault was a little more subtle and happened further down the line, usually just as the sketch was starting to be rehearsed. As Artistic Director, he would become concerned that the sketch was "too Mad Magazine," it didn't "fit into the Chucklehead universe," or that it was too regressive–too reminiscent of the "old Chucklehead scripts." Sometimes his girlfriend had a problem with it.

I would sit at the script meetings, gradually draining a six pack. The beer would dissolve the disappointment in my gut so that, eventually, I just didn't care anymore.

Slowly, for me, the script writing process had changed. Only months ago, I had run out of ideas that really excited me, and scriptwriting became a soulless exercise. The only thing that kept me going was the conviction that if I stopped writing, I would fade out of the group, and that the moment I was gone, they would all become rich and famous without me. We all felt that way. It was what kept us together.

I started to watch what mechanics worked in other people's scripts: Peter, who worked at *Games* magazine, wrote skits that were essentially puzzles with characters in them. Judy's scripts were inhabited by phony, shallow and pathetic "cool" characters.

Russell skewered yuppies and wrote scathing parodies of modern plays. They all stole shamelessly from me and I stole shamelessly from them.

Scripts had to be hip and topical and timely. They had to build and reach a climax, and there had to be a little twist or coda at the end. And, of course, if you really wanted to get the script through, you could use one of the actors' favorite and recurring characters. All these agendas swirled through my head every time I sat down at the keyboard. That's how I came to keystroke in three pages worth of letters and punctuation adding up to that pointless, lingering little brain fart I titled, "Black Hole of Fun."

A friend of mine had once described a woman whose negativity could destroy any party she attended and called her "The Black Hole of Fun." Spanky had a character named Droopy, whom he had based on the dour dog cartoon character, also named Droopy, who looked and spoke exactly like Spanky's character, Droopy. So, I put Droopy in a cocktail party situation, where he killed the mood with his increasingly negative lines. The resulting sketch was just as stale and stagnant as the party after Droopy's arrival. The only reason it got through the review process was that Russell was absent the night it was read, and Spanky naturally campaigned for it since his last Droopy sketch got put to pasture.

The audience began to trickle in to the Judith Anderson Theatre. Most of them were vaguely familiar to me, friends of other writers and cast members. Friends of friends of friends. And occasional strangers. Then I noticed two faces that filled me heart with warmth–John and Sonya Fiarello.

I'd met them at Club Med in Guadeloupe just two months earlier. I was already drunk when I was seated with a table-full of strangers at dinner and didn't particularly feel like talking to this clean-cut, ambitious Turk and his doting little trophy wife. Somehow, in the initially barren conversation, references to esoteric movies and books began to bloom. Soon we were volleying literary and cinematic allusions furiously back and between us like ruthless Chinese ping pong players. Then Sonya noticed my copy of *The Thin Man* in my beach bag. "John and I love Dashiell Hammett," she said, placing her hands down on my forearm for emphasis.

"His sentences are as hard and short and uncompromising as a slug from a forty-five," I said. "Wouldn't it be great know people like Nick and Nora Charles?"

"It'd be even greater to be Nick and Nora Charles," Sonya countered. That's when I realized they really *were* Nick and Nora Charles–smart, witty, urbane New Yorkers who took up with hard-drinking, unsavory characters like myself

"You better watch out," I said, my face flushing from too much sun and alcohol and intimacy. "I like to collect exceptional people."

"John and I are pretty big people collectors ourselves," Sonya responded, winking.

I spent the rest of the vacation tagging along with them. Having every meal with them. Sailing with them. Drinking with them. John was an investment banker of Northern Italian descent who, despite 12-hour days, managed to read several books a week. Sonya, with dark Russian hair and eyes, worked in advertising and read even more than John. Her psychic Russian grandmother had told her the moment she met John that he would someday become her husband. They had been all over the world, seen everything, done everything. And they were so excited to meet someone who worked in Theatre.

As we parted company, we traded phone numbers and I told them I'd invite them to a Chucklehead show, which seemed to excite them. As soon as the *Vogue* article came out, with the headline "They'll Take Manhattan," I came home to a message on my answering machine: "Hi, Rob. It's Sonya Fiarello. I just read that review in *Vogue,* and I just wanted to say, well, congratulations! We look forward to seeing your show and hope we can get together afterwards."

And here they were. They came down the aisle and each gave me a big hug. They introduced me to their friends Alan, an even more cleancut broker who shook my hand with an incredulous and suspicious look on his face, and short-haired Sharon, who looked as if she were witnessing a gruesome car accident.

That was okay. If they were friends of John and Sonya, they were all right in my book.

"Rob's the one we were talking about. He's one of the writers" John explained to the other couple.

"Do you have anything in this show?" Sonya asked.

"Yeah but, you know, it's really a collaborative effort," I said, sounding oh-so-modest. Sonya sat down next to me, John next to her, and the other couple next to him. They continued chatting amongst themselves, but I was having a hard time hearing the conversation, much less following it, my eyes darting around nervously.

As the lights came down, Sonya patted my forearm and whispered, "Don't worry. It's going to be great. I can sense these things."

As the first video came up, I started to worry about the two TVs on either side of the stage. Could you hear them okay? Could you even see them well enough from our angle? But everyone seemed to be laughing.

As the first skit, Judy's "Suburban Transmedium," came up, I noticed something else: The stage was huge, nothing like the cozy little stage at the West Bank. The actors seemed so tiny up there, like a few people holding a quiet, private little conversation in some corner of Grand Central Station. Angie was playing a New Age lady visiting a seemingly phony, chain-smoking medium (Rose) to find out about her past lives.

Suddenly, just as the audience is convinced she's a fake, she begins speaking in the thundering male voice of Oreo, a male African warrior (Spanky on a backstage mike). Rose and Spanky were so totally attuned to each other that you were firmly convinced it was her own voice. The male African warrior proceeds to piss off the New Age lady–and lose the medium a client–by describing just how insignificant her past lives were: "They say it took ten thousand slaves to build the pyramids–and you were one of them! Blaaaaaah!"

It worked, even in that overwhelming space. The audience didn't guffaw, but they laughed at the appropriate times.

In "The Theatregoers," which was Peter's, two high-brow couples (Rick and Angie, and Dirk and Rose) are coming home from the theatre. The tweedy Dirk character, smoking a pipe, is completely tearing the show apart, and Rose explains to the other couple that nothing measures up him anymore, ever since he saw Lee J. Cobb in "Death of a Salesman" in the 1950s. Dirk starts to reminisce about the show and what a great performance Lee J. Cobb gave and how no modern-day actor could match it. "And I'll never figure out how he did that thing with his head!"

"You always bring that up, but I can never remember that part!" Rose snaps, cringing and downing her entire glass of wine.

"I don't know how he did it," Dirk continues, "But his head just got really, really big, like a hundred times its normal size, and it floated out over the audience. And just when it looked like it was going to get too big, it just . . . stopped. I've never seen anything like it!"

The audience laughed and continued to laugh as Rose and the other couple dealt with their increasing discomfort. When the skit blacked out, they applauded enthusiastically. We had 'em.

As the next video came on, I patted Sonya on the forearm and whispered, "Back in a few."

My legs were simultaneously rigid and rubbery, and it was extremely difficult maneuvering my way between the seats to get to the outer aisle. I quietly stumbled back to the lobby, feeling the kind of shakiness I always got when I was about to throw up, ambled from door to door, found the door I was looking for, and followed the labyrinth of corridors and staircases to back stage. I was due to appear in my own sketch, "Black Hole of Fun," as a guest at the cocktail party. It had been a couple of years since I'd appeared on stage, and even then, I had stage fright. Now I had what could only be described as stage dread. Why did I have to write that damn sketch in the first place?

It had also been two years since I had been backstage during a performance, and it was a whole other world. It was a hive. The actors were all transformed into worker bees, maneuvering back and forth past each other in a way that looked totally random to the untrained observer, but was actually very focused and purposeful. Dirk and Spanky moved three folding chairs onto the stage and draped a blanket over it to make it look like a sofa. Rose put on a table holding several glasses of red-colored liquid and a plate of plastic sushi. Spanky took off a costume from a previous sketch, and underneath it were the gray pants, white shirt, suspenders and bow tie that made up his Droopy outfit. Rose whipped off her baggy dress, underneath which was a black evening gown, and put the dress down on the three folding chairs that comprised her dressing room. Two feet away, Spanky grabbed his big, black Droopy glasses from his own prop bag and put them on. Next to him, Pat removed a Hawaiian shirt to reveal a white button-down shirt with its sleeves rolled up. He unrolled the sleeves, buttoned the cuffs, and threw on a dinner jacket.

Five feet away, Angie pulled off her shirt, underneath which was nothing. Nothing except those breasts that I had often visualized, but which far exceeded my wildest fantasies. In no particular hurry, she put on a party dress and adjusted it. My eyes began to water.

Pat, moving past behind me, patted me on the shoulder in

a comforting way. "Look away, Rob, before you turn into a pillar of salt," he whispered.

The video ended. My dreaded sketch was about to begin. Panic set in. I could no longer think straight. As both a writer and an actor, I felt doubly exposed. The real actors—and Peter, who was another walk-on—moved toward the front of the stage, but I was trapped on flypaper. With a clap of thunder, everything went black.

A hand grabbed my sweaty palm in the darkness, put a glass into my free hand, and pulled me gently onto stage. With another clap of thunder, the lights came up. They were blinding and warm. I was in the middle of some kind of cocktail party, and Rick was standing beside me, smiling reassuringly. In the direction of the audience, I could see only darkness. I quickly took a gulp of my wine to calm myself down, only to discover it was actually water with red food coloring.

The actors all began quietly muttering things to each other. I forced a smile and pretended to speak to Rick. Dirk and Rose began speaking to Spanky in a louder tone of voice. He said something back. Their words sounded vaguely familiar—only something about what Spanky was saying was all wrong. Some words were out of order and the rhythm was askew.

Rick was saying something to me, actually saying real words to me and trying to communicate real thoughts. This new development startled the hell out of me. What could he possibly have to say to me now, up on stage, in the middle of a skit? "What?" I mouthed at him. "What did you say?"

"Are you listening? Spanky is completely butchering his lines," he said gleefully. As I was still processing this statement, and why it was so important that he tell me this while we were up on stage in the middle of a show, Rick reached over to the table, picked up the plate of sushi, and said in his stage voice, "Sushi, anyone?"

"You can get liver parasites from that stuff!" Spanky said.

From off in the darkness beyond the stage, I heard a few titters. What were they laughing at? The line? Was it actually working?

More things were said. Rick leaned into me and muttered in my ear, "Say your line!"

Line? Oh yeah, line. "Hey, there's a Don Rickles film festival down at the Waverly," I said loudly, my voice quivering. "Does anyone want to come with me?" The audience laughed. Something worked. Maybe the line? Maybe the way I said it?

"I do!" said various cocktail party attendees. Rick put his hand on my shoulder and gently guided me off stage with the others. "Good job," Rick whispered as he maneuvered me off stage.

Spanky said one final thing, the coda that served as the period at the end of the skit, and the lights went down with a clap. The audience applauded–not emphatically, but they applauded. I heaved a sigh of relief. The sketch didn't bomb, and I didn't bomb.

I sighed. My panic was now replaced with an adrenaline high. I jogged back through the labyrinth to the lobby, and then quietly sneaked back down the aisle, between the seats, and into my rightful place beside Sonya. I was there several seconds before she noticed me with a start. "Hey, you were great!" she whispered. "Did you by any chance write it?"

"I'm not sure."

Sonya looked at me quizzically out of the corner of her eyes. The video faded, and I knew that Peter's "Special Ed" skit was coming up. It absolutely killed us the night it was read–even Russell liked it–but it had never been put in front of an audience before. It was a clever puzzle that, when solved, made a wry and touching statement about the human condition. When the lights came up on Angie with a thunderclap, her eyes never narrowed from that glassy stare. From the audience, it was as if you could tell her pupils weren't contracting either. There was a knock. "Come in!" she said, her eyes unwavering.

Dirk and Rose, playing a yuppie couple, came in and started talking to her. They were complaining that their daughter felt neglected in class. The Angie character asked them their daughter's name. When they told her the girl's name, she said she didn't have anyone by that name in her class. Angrily, they said she'd been in the class for months, and what the hell was going on? "We had a girl by that name signed up for class, but she never answered roll call."

"Didn't you see her signing you from the back of the room?"

Signing?"

"She's a deaf-mute! Isn't this a class for the deaf?"

"No, it's a class for the blind!" said Angie.

"You mean you're–"

"Yes. Totally blind. Can't see a thing," Angie said, never wavering from that trance-like stare, but now conveying a sad horror. Her acting was much, much too convincing. "You mean, she's been in class the whole time? Oh my God! That's where that rapping sound has been coming from! I just thought the radiator was broken!"

That was perhaps the best punchline in the skit. I started to snicker. Sonya flinched and studied me out of the corner of her eye. That's when I realized not a single one of the sixty-plus audience members was laughing, chuckling, snickering, snorting, tittering, or making any sound whatsoever. A cold draft blew through the audience. Oh my God! Sketch alert! Bomb! Bomb! Bomb!

It was worse than a bomb. For the past two years, all of us had taken great delight in skipping back and forth along the borders of good taste. Yet, through this innocent, well-intentioned little puzzle sketch, sweet, good-natured Peter had wandered blindly over the line and into the Land of the Unforgivable. What were we thinking?

I wanted to crawl out of the theatre. I turned and looked at Peter, sitting in the back of the audience. He leaned forward and covered his face with his hands. Then I looked at Angie, Dirk, and Rose, trapped on stage and having to say the remainder of those lines, with the full knowledge that they were digging deeper and deeper graves for themselves.

The sketch ended. No applause, not even polite applause. Nothing.

Most of the audience members stuck it out. More sketches happened, to very sparse laughter and applause. When the whole thing was over, there was muted applause. John, Sonya, and the other couple stood up. They started to file out, gaze low, when Sonya turned slowly toward me. "Thanks for inviting us!" she said, with a sad smile, patting me on the shoulder, and the four of them left the theater.

I never saw them again.

ROB DINSMOOR

RAID ON THE EAST VILLAGE

The script meeting was winding down and my heart was sinking at the prospect of the dreadful task before us. "Does anyone have any more scripts to read?" Dirk asked pleadingly. We all looked around. No one did.

With a lock of red hair falling over her right eye, Rose was busily stirring a big bucket of glue, looking like some overworked Irish mother stirring Mulligan stew. Pat tore open a large brown paper parcel from the printer, and from it he pulled stacks of 24" by 30" Chucklehead posters for our next gig at the West Bank, "Nuclear Winter Wonderland." The centerpiece of each poster was *the* Chucklehead, a big, crudely rendered, fat, scary face in a paroxysm of laughter. It was such a big, in-your-face face that you couldn't help but notice it from half a block away.

Originally, the Chucklehead logo had been a line drawing of some 1950s clean-cut father icon wearing a crown that Paul had taken from his extensive weird old clip art collection. But since Pat himself co-owned a mail-order adult comic book and pornography outlet, he knew all the ins and outs of quality print jobs and eventually took over the printing of our promotional posters and postcards. Soon after he took over these new responsibilities, he abruptly switched our logo.

He had taken a tiny, grainy printed photo of a big, fat man's laughing face from an article on the therapeutic effect of laughter, and had blown it up by about 10,000%. This enlargement turned the photo's dot matrix into a wild bunch of tiny circles that crudely reconstructed the man's face in an eerie way. Coincidentally or not, the official Chucklehead bore a strong resemblance to Pat's face. And since Pat often introduced and closed the show, as a kind of emcee, it would have been reasonable for audience members to conclude that he really was the chuckle-head of the Chucklehead, much as Deborah Harry was the blonde in Blondie. Score one for Pat!

I slipped a bunch of posters into my backpack. As usual, Pat immediately swept up Angie and Rose, picking Rick to complete the team. All three always seemed eager to join Pat's team for reasons that escaped me. Unfortunately, I was stuck on Dirk's team along with Spanky and Judy. I would much rather have been at home in my dry, warm apartment with a six pack, watching movies like "I Drink Your Blood" or "I Spit on Your Grave."

We all left Rose and Remy's West Village apartment together and walked due east. The March night air was intolerably damp and cold, refusing to yield even an inch to the oncoming spring.

Tonight's target was the East Village, which had the great-est square footage of bare walls and construction site fences and naturally attracted posters like flies on manure. The East Village, we thought, was also frequented by the greatest number per capita of potential Chucklehead audience members–hip, smart, young peo-ple who were as angry at the world as we were. Our people didn't actually live there, but they liked to slum down there, eating in trendy restaurants and going to gritty new wave bars.

Pat's team headed due south and would start postering from 6th Street up. Our team was working its way down from 14th Street, with the tacit understanding that we would quit when the two groups met somewhere in the middle, or we started encoun-tering Chucklehead posters we hadn't put up.

"Jesus fucking Christ, it's cold," Dirk bitched as we com-menced to wallpaper our first construction board at the corner of Second Avenue and 13th Street. As Judy played nervous lookout, Dirk slopped a swatch of glue on the wood, I drew a poster from my backpack like an archer pulling an arrow from his quiver, Spanky and I slapped it against the wall, and Dirk sealed it on by slopping more glue on the poster—and my hand. The glue was not only sticky but also stingingly cold.

"Ow, shit, Dirk. Watch out!"

"Sorry," he said so dismissively that I knew it was going to happen again and again. Damn, I hated postering. And Dirk.

Meanwhile, Spanky tried to keep us entertained with one of his running character monologues. This time it was his Southeast Asian pimp, and he was clearly improvising. "Okay, you Chuckahead. You so funny! Enough funny, you go put up posta now! Chop chop! When you done with dat, you go inside and make boom-boom with customa. You make good suckee-fuckee, eh, Chuckahead? You mouth so pletty! Wait a minute, now, Chuckahead. You bend over fo' me now! Hode still now, don't move! Yeah, Chuckahead, you soooo good!" And so on and so forth, exploring this theme in its endless permutations.

"What's the matter, man? You look really irritated," Dirk said to me. His tone of voice was more accusatory than solicitous.

"Nothing," I said. "It's just that some of the ambient noise is starting to get on my nerves."

We wove our way down Second Avenue, venturing down the side streets just far enough to put some posters on any spare walls, dumpsters, or telephone poles we could find. "Get the lead out, man!" Dirk said to me at one point. "You're a little slow on the draw!"

"That's because you glued my fingers together, you care-less fuck!"

Virtually the entire free surface of the East Village was wall-papered with other posters—one-man shows, gay and lesbian coffee houses, off-off-off-Broadway productions, and punk bands like Thalidomide Babies, Jizzum Trail, and the Skidmarks. Through a sort of cultural natural selection, most of these bands and troupes and coffee houses would disappear within months. Nothing ever survived very long. Nonetheless, as a matter of etiquette, we rarely covered up other posters unless the advertised event had come and gone.

We came across a poster for Jennifer Lane's upcoming gig at the Greene Street Café. She was a thirty-something cabaret singer whose voice and disposition were like molasses with glass ground up in it. She'd been one of the chorus girls in "Little Shop of Horrors" at the Orpheum, but acted as if she'd starred in her own Broadway show. Months ago, we had a short gig directly after her at the Greene Street Café. As we came into the waiting area with our stuff and an audience bigger than hers, she pointed to us from the stage and said "Oh, look, here come those little Chuckleheads with their little wigs, their little costumes, and their little shoes. I'm gonna come see y'all some night. Not tonight and probably not next week, but some night!"

Dirk, Spanky, and I looked at each other, thinking the same thought at once. Dirk slapped the glue brush against the photo of her face, and Spanky and I pressed our poster against her face like a pillow. Then Dirk slopped on more glue, sealing her in.

Judy strolled over to us, her hands in her pockets, looking very nervous and self-conscious. "Hey, guys. Cool it. There's a police car coming along Twelfth Street."

Dirk picked up the bucket and carried it in his left hand to obscure it from the street. I was just some dude with a backpack and Spanky was a completely innocent bystander. Judy looked nervous but what nice, white, middle-class young lady wouldn't look nervous walking alone in that neighborhood? We were just four unremarkable, law-abiding New Yorkers who just happened to be walking in the same direction in the same general vicinity—hopefully blending in to the heavy pedestrian traffic down Second Avenue.

"Yo! You! Get your ass over here!" It was coming from the

passenger's side of the cop car, which had pulled to the curb on Second Avenue. Suddenly I felt as if a squirrel were trying to claw its way out of my ribcage. "I want a word with you!"

Fortunately, he was addressing a young Hispanic man in a trench coat 10 feet behind us. "I thought I told you to stay off this block . . ." the cop continued and soon we were out of earshot.

On Tenth Street, we found the Holy Grail of postering walls. It was 20 feet wide and 10 feet high. There were other posters there, but they were old. We had quite a few posters left and would not mind terribly if we ran out of them fairly quickly. Soon we would reconnoiter with the Pat squad who would be advancing from the South. Time for a blitzkrieg.

Dirk began painting a wide swatch of glue at about forehead height, covering most of the horizontal distance of the wall. I fed the posters to Judy and Spanky, who pressed them against the wall, side by side. As soon as we had a row of 10, Dirk would lumber back around and simultaneously seal in the posters and make a new swatch of glue below the first row. And so on, splattering glue all over everyone's hands, clothes, and shoes.

About midway through the second row, a large hand came down firmly but gently on my shoulders and turned me around. It was a cop, about six and a half feet tall and 250 pounds. The brim of his hat cast a shadow that almost completely obscured his face. The squirrel in my ribcage fainted dead away. "Is it really worth it?" he asked in a thick Queens accent. "I mean, how much could they possibly be paying you to do this?"

Spanky came over with a grin on his face and laughed in his boyishly self-effacing manner. "Hey, you know what? Nobody's paying us to do this! We're all part of this comedy troupe called Chucklehead and this is for our next show." He crinkled his nose and added, "The show's okay, except one or two of the sketches are really, really bad!"

Spanky to the rescue. The cop just stared at him in disbelief.

"What you're doing is called defacing public property," the cop said. "Your show is going to be over in a few weeks, but the poster is going to be up here much longer than that, making the neighborhood look like crap."

Who was he kidding? First of all, the neighborhood was inhabited mostly by dealers, junkies, winos, homeless people, punk rockers, and the occasional prostitute. Most of them didn't care what the neighborhood looked like and the punk rockers actually preferred it that way. Furthermore, this poster would disappear in a matter of days underneath the hundreds of other posters and leaflets that fluttered onto the walls and stuck to them like flypaper. It was a cultural jungle out there, it was survival of the fittest, and if our posters weren't seen, Chucklehead would perish. "Yes, officer," I responded.

"With all due respect, officer, it's not like this is the Upper East Side or something," Dirk said, with a hint of a whine in his voice. "I mean, look at it. Who lives here except punk rockers and drug dealers and homeless people?"

As he was saying this, I was looking directly at a little deli across the street with Hebrew letters across it. It was the type of place that served bagels, blintzes, and matza ball soup to the little old Russian Jewish couples who had inhabited the area for decades.

"My mother lives in this neighborhood," the cop informed him flatly.

"Dirk, you schmuck! You total putz! What were you thinking?" I chimed in. Judy, who really was Jewish, stared at me in such a way as to tell me not to push it.

"We're really sorry, officer," Dirk said, looking like a rebellious teenager trying to dodge the wrath of his Junior High School principal.

"Let me see that bucket," the cop said and Dirk handed it to him. "You know what I'm going to do with it?"

"We're really sorry, officer," Judy repeated. "At least no one was hurt."

"I'm going to do nothing with it. You're going to pour it out because you're generally law-abiding citizens and you have respect for my mother's neighborhood." He handed it back to Dirk, who dutifully and daintily poured it into the street next to the curb.

"Well done. Now, if I catch you out doing the same thing tonight, I'll give you a citation for defacing public property and that glue is going on your heads. Got it?" We all nodded. "Good night, gentlemen, and lady."

"*Mazel tov!*" I muttered, as we parted ways.

"Well, fuck. I guess that's it for the night," Dirk said, sounding almost as relieved as disappointed. The four of us dispersed. Dirk took the empty glue bucket and he and Spanky decided to share a cab uptown, dropping Judy at the PATH station on the way so she could take her train back to Hoboken. I kept the posters and headed South toward the West 4th Street stop.

It began to snow the kind of snow that melts on your skin and clothes on contact, making them cold and wet and penetrating to the bone. I squinted as they landed on my eyeballs. It was adding insult to injury. God, I hated March.

That's when I heard a sweet melodic trio singing, "I'm Dreaming of a White Christmas." I turned to see Pat, Rose, and Angie dancing up the other side of Second Avenue. I crossed the street to join them.

"Rob!" Pat cried out. "Merry Christmas, you poor lost waif! What happened to your crew?"

"We got busted."

"I'm sorry to hear that," Pat responded, and then his face suddenly lit up. "Is Dirk by any chance behind bars? Surrounded by large black men who want to make him their bitch?"

"No."

Pat's shoulders fell forward in mock disappointment and he said, "I'm sorry to hear that, too."

"What happened to Rick?"

"He had to go," Pat explained. "I hereby anoint you an honorary member of the Pat team. And as such, you shall drink of the sacramental Pat whiskey."

From his pocket, Pat pulled a flask of Glenn Livet and extended it to me. It went down smoothly and instantly my cold and bitterness were replaced by a warm spiritual glow. I held it out to the others, and all three took ceremonial nips. Our eyes glowed with yuletide joy and we began to sing "Jingle Bells."

This time, I was the lookout, and I tried to emulate the guys who played look-out for the Three Card Monte games. Alternately, I acted like I was waiting to hail a cab, reading a poster, looking into a store window, or waiting impatiently for someone.

The Pat team's modus operandi was roughly the same as the Dirk team's but was choreographed with precision, focus, clarity, and joy. With the zeal of Jackson Pollack, Pat applied the glue with fierce passion yet control. He strutted down the street, flanked by the two beauties, like a Big and Tall Man's Tony Orlando and Dawn. With the showy deliberation of a magic act, Angie and Rose withdrew posters one at a time, let the entire back of the poster kiss the wall simultaneously, and caressed the front of the poster until it became part of the wall.

Their aesthetic sense was much better than the Dirk team's had been. Instead of seeing how many they could plaster to the wall, they made beautiful mosaics of varying shapes and sizes, always taking into consideration the size and shape of the surface they were dealing with. For the first time, I realized that postering needn't be just a chore, it could be a form of art.

When we were done, Pat offered to take us all home in the Patmobile. He dropped Angie and Rose right at their respective doorsteps in the West Village. Since he, too, lived in Brooklyn, he was more than happy to deliver me home safely to Sheepshead Bay. "It's all part of the Pat package," he explained. "As a self-employed small businessman, the backbone of this great nation of ours, I have learned to strive for excellence in all my pursuits."

A couple of nights later, I happened to be in the East Village and decided to check in on our handiwork. There was no sign of our posters anywhere. Already they were covered with fresh posters still wet with glue.

I RODE WITH A MANIAC

Against a backdrop of blue sky and brilliant white clouds, the cables of the Brooklyn Bridge rifled across my field of vision, crisscrossing each other in a moiré pattern worthy of a Pink Floyd laser show. The sun radiated on my face as warm air rustled past my ears and the Watchtower Building raced toward us at the end of the bridge.

Rick had rented this convertible–a red convertible, no less–with Chucklehead funds so that we could pick up a second-hand TV in upstate New York and drop it off at the West Bank Café. Now that we were done, Rick was more than willing to drive me back to my apartment in exchange for a lobster dinner in Sheepshead Bay, and I was more than willing to be driven. I was actually ecstatic at the prospect of being driven back to my apartment like a human being rather than going home through dark, underground tunnels like some kind of burrowing rodent.

The only downside was that sometimes Rick got on my nerves. His mouth rattled on like a machine gun, spraying bullets in all directions, sometimes grazing the people around him.

On top of that, sometimes he gave me this sense of impending danger. Every week, it seemed, he had a deeply unsettling story in which he would be minding his own business and total strangers would lash out, persecute him, or beat him up for no apparent reason. And it was becoming more and more apparent that he was actually a sort of magnet for trouble.

I was trying to just be in the moment when a loud, juiced-up Trans Am passed us on the left. That's when Rick leaned his head out the window and barked. The large, thick-necked, crew-cut guy at the wheel glared at Rick for a moment, jammed his foot on the accelerator, and–fortunately–disappeared into the distance. "You know, some day you're going to bark at the wrong guy–and he's going to shoot you or run you off the road."

"You worry too much," Rick said.

When we got off the Belt Parkway, Rick took Shore Drive away from my apartment building and toward the Bay proper. Because it was a beautiful summer day, it was teeming with life. People were fishing off the footbridge that spanned the small bay, and richly tanned people milled about in tank tops, shorts, and sandals. When Rick spotted a particularly slender olive-skinned male in his early twenties, he reached out his hand and said, much too loudly, "Boy, I'd like to strap him to my face for about a week!"

"Jesus, Rick! You're going to get the shit kicked out of you one of these days," I said.

"No, look. That guy is definitely queer as they come."

"He looked perfectly straight to me," I said.

"Trust me on this. You don't have the radar that I have. I can spot 'em from a mile off."

We parked. He got up on the seat and vaulted over the convertible door without opening it, nearly knocking into a tanned guy and his tough-sexy, gum-smacking girlfriend, and said, "Ta da!" The couple looked vaguely flustered but, fortunately, kept walking. As the guy walked away, Rick made no secret of checking out the guy's ass.

The restaurant was huge and packed with old Russian-Jewish immigrants, Italian-Americans of all ages, and young urban professional tourists of all ethnicities. It was the best-known restaurant in Sheepshead Bay and reputedly owned by The Mob. At the end of the bar were a few heavy old men in rumpled seats, smoking cigars. Seated at the end of the bar was a man I assumed to be a bouncer, or worse, who looked big and beefy enough to punch out bears. The front of the restaurant was wide open and the air was thick with garlic, butter, brine, the rattling of silverware, and the roar of dozens of conversations competing in volume.

Once we were seated, the waitress appeared. She was blonde, pleasingly plump, and scrubbed-looking, with a makeshift ponytail. "Can I get you anything?" she asked.

"You mean, besides you?" he asked, giving her this remarkably entranced look with his trademark angelic eyes.

I had no idea how she would react, but she just grinned, actually blushed a little, and said, "I'll come back when you're ready."

"But I'm ready for you now, sweetheart!"

"Stop it!" she said, but she was still grinning. It was something I envied about Rick. He apparently could say stuff like that and pull it off. If I ever said something like that, the waitress would have called the cops.

"We'll have two Becks," I finally said, grinning.

"Got it. And while I'm getting your drinks, please feel free to take advantage of the salad bar."

At the salad bar, I put together a veritable compost heap on my plate. When I returned to the table, Rick was still carefully composing a little salad with great finesse. That's when the restaurant erupted with the sound of barking. Everyone, including the waitress and the bouncer, looked around to see where the dog was or at least where the barking was coming from. His back turned to the room, Rick continued to look as if he were methodically composing his salad, but I knew better. I had to admit the boy had talent.

Rick finally returned with a small salad and the waitress returned with our beers. "What, are you running a kennel here?" he asked, with mock indignation.

"Sometimes I think so, with some of the customers we get around here," she answered, winking at him.

"How big are your biggest lobsters?" Rick asked.

"Three pounds."

"We'll take 'em," I said.

Rick thrust his Becks bottle into mine with so much gusto I was surprised they didn't shatter. "Thanks, buddy," he said, gulped down about half the bottle, and alluding to the movie "Barfly," called out, "To my frieeeeends!"

Rick quickly finished his salad and returned to the salad bar, not because he was that hungry but because it was now his stage. He suddenly started sniffling loudly and blinking his eyes, and I knew what was coming next: The old stage sneeze on the salad bar. That would get us thrown out for sure—or worse.

Rick was closing his eyes, gasping in air through a gaping mouth and going "Aaah . . . aah . . . aaah," when he was distracted by the arrival of a fat, stooped-over little old man with an unlit stub of a cigar protruding from the corner of his jowls.

Resting a plate on his protruding stomach, the old man began loading it with potato salad. Rick's eyes widened with glee, and he turned back to the salad bar. When he turned around again, his own jowls were suddenly puffed out—with God knows what—and he had a baby carrot sticking out the corner of his mouth. Then he was hunched over, standing directly behind the old man, mimicking his every move to perfection. A young couple at a near-by table started laughing. The old man turned back to see what they were laughing at, and suddenly the couple stopped laughing and Rick was standing tall again. As soon as the man turned back to the salad bar, Rick went back to his routine, miming the slopping of potato salad onto his plate.

As the man lumbered back toward the barstool, Rick lumbered behind him part of the way, and then veered off to come to our table. As the man sat down at the barstool, the bouncer was glaring in our direction. Rick looked over at the bouncer, daintily peeled his polo shirt down his shoulder, and gave him a pouting, sultry look.

What if the old man was one of the mob bosses that owned the place? Was the bouncer his bodyguard? What was to become of us? Dread settled in my stomach along with the lobster and beer.

"Rick, you have to quit pulling that shit."

"What shit?"

We finished the first beers and ordered another round. When the lobsters arrived, they were huge, looking like red armadillos. Rick hummed in gratitude, banging the top of his shell cracker on the table top, ripped off one of the claws, and opened the back of it with an ear-splitting crack, sending saltwater spraying into my face and possibly onto the people at the next table. But I was hungry, I loved lobster, I had a beer under my belt, the storm clouds had passed, and I no longer cared, so I ripped into my lobster with the same degree of gusto. Pretty soon, Rick and I were in a speed-eating contest, cramming the sweet lobster meat into our faces without the slightest bit of self-consciousness.

Within twenty minutes, we were both full, we were on our third beers, the table was littered with body parts of lobsters, and I felt as if I had just swum in the ocean at low tide. Rick grabbed the lobster antennae, pressed them into his forehead, turned to the couple at the nearby table, and said, "Take me to your leader!" Not only did they laugh, but so did a number of people around the room. As the waitress walked by, Rick reached out with one of the lobster claws and mimed pinching her ass with it. People laughed, she turned around to see what he was doing, and gave him a look of amused exasperation.

We finished off with canolis, got our bill, and I laid my Visa card inside the leather folder of the bill. Rick filled his mouth with canole and said in his best—and loudest Brando voice, "Don Tattaglia, I have considered your generous offer and am now telling you I must refuse it."

At that point, I didn't think any mob bosses in the room would care what we were doing. They had bigger fish to try, and we were entertaining the customers—good for business, right? And so I responded, loudly, "Don Corleone, may I ask your reasons?"

"Because drugs are a dirty business. The Corleone family has many friends who are judges and other people in high places. And they would not be our friends any longer if our business was drugs. But I wish you great fortune in your endeavors," Rick responded.

"Excuse me," the waitress said, tapping me on the shoulder, looking very concerned. "I'm afraid your card didn't go through."

I then realized that I must have maxed it out buying my computer three weeks earlier. "Sorry about that. I'll pay in cash."

Just then, the bouncer showed up, gave me a really dirty look, and said to the waitress, "Everything okay over here?"

"Everything's fine," I snapped at him. "My credit card didn't clear so I'm paying cash."

I opened my wallet to discover a total of $30, nothing close to what we owed.

"Is there a Chase ATM machine around here?" I asked.

"About ten blocks away, but you're not going anywhere," the bouncer said, stepping right between me and the door, folding arms that were as big as my legs. I knew he was dying to split our heads open and here was his excuse.

"If I can't get to the bank, how the hell am I supposed to pay, Einstein?" I growled, and then winced when I realized what I'd said. Just as he was unfolding his arms and reaching them out, there was a crashing sound as Rick stood up suddenly, grabbing at his own throat and toppling the chair from under him. His face turned red, his eyes were bugging out of their sockets. With his left hand, he held his throat and with his right index finger, he pointed to it, trying desperately to mouth words.

"Can't you see he's choking here? Doesn't anyone know the Heimlich maneuver?"

The bouncer came up behind Rick, wrapped his arms

around him in the Heimlich maneuver, and said, "You'd better not be faking this, asshole!"

Suddenly, the canoli shot from Rick's mouth, followed by an acrid red and yellow geyser that christened the table. The bouncer let go, Rick coughed a few times and then began taking labored breaths. "Jesus Christ!" he said, and then turned to the bouncer. "You saved my life!"

Half an hour later, I had the wheel and we were driving back to my apartment building. I felt strangely exhilarated again.

While Rick had recuperated at the table, tacitly serving as a hostage, I had jogged down to the Chase ATM and back. I had given the waitress a thirty percent tip, and Rick had again thanked the bouncer loudly and publicly for saving his life.

"Jesus, that had to be the most convincing act I've ever seen," I told him in the car. "I'm surprised you didn't spin your head around and speak in tongues!"

"It started out as an act, but once that big scumbag got hold of me—well, the projectile vomiting really wasn't my idea." Gasping for breath, he said, "Christ, I think he broke a rib!"

As we pulled up to my apartment building, Rick said, "Hey, can I stop up for a minute? I've got to take a leak."

I hesitated for a second, because the place was such a mess, but finally agreed. How could I turn down such a request? He came up to my apartment, the Fortress of Solitude, into which no other human being had entered in the past year. As we entered, he looked at the strange little scar in my door frame and said, "The previous tenants were Jewish. They had a mezuzah."

"What?"

"There used to be a mezuzah here. It's a handwritten scroll from the Old Testament. It's placed in the doorway to protect the household from evil."

As we entered the apartment, and he looked around at my chaos and clutter, he said, "Oh. Too late, I guess."

After he had finished in the bathroom, it was my turn, and Rick began looking over the dusty video collection that I had accumulated over the last two years. My tastes ran to the dark and macabre, including "The Terminator" and lots of Alfred Hitchcock. "Say," he said. "Did you ever see that bizarre movie where this guy sells his soul to a sinister company in exchange for a new life as an artist, who's played by Rock Hudson? I can't remember the name of it, but it had this creepy music and these really claustrophobic close-up shots."

"It's 'Seconds,'" I said, and pulled it from my video library. "Written by David Eli and directed by none other than John Frankenheimer."

"Oh. My. God!" he said. "I can't believe you have that. Can we watch it?"

"Of course," I said. I cracked another beer, he lit up a joint, and, as the sun set over the Belt Parkway, we watched the whole dark, disturbing thing from beginning to end.

THE LONG, SLOW RIDE
TO BROOKLYN

Go home, Rob," Jim kept repeating from his bed, his voice
never wavering in volume or pitch. "Go home."

I turned and walked out the door of the apartment. As I
quietly descended the stairs, I could hear Angie's voice, fading in
the distance. "You can't just turn him out like this! It's cold! It's rain-
ing! It's late! It's a long way to Sheepshead Bay and he can barely
walk!"

I stepped out onto the stoop and was immediately hit with
a wall of water. By the time I got to the end of their street, I was
soaked.

The way back to the subway at West 4th had never
seemed so long and so tortuous. I had just gotten to the point
where I could negotiate the West Village sober, but drunk it was
still a cruel maze. I hit that odd tear in the time-space continuum
where West 4th intersects with West 10th Street. It wasn't until a
number of blocks later that I realized I'd wound up on West 10th
instead of West 4th and had to wait till I reached 6th Avenue before
heading south again toward West 4th.

Still, it didn't really matter. I couldn't get any wetter.

The day had taken one unexpected turn after another. We
were early on in rehearsing out next show. From the previous script
reading meetings, we had chosen five skits that we were definitely
going to put up for the next show, and I was happy that two of
them were mine. The rest would probably be old standbys. Life
was good—except that when we showed up at the rehearsal space
we had rented on West 44th Street, the door was locked.

Dirk found a pay phone and tried calling the guy in charge of renting the space, and got his answering machine. His California surfer dude persona now had an edge to it: "Artie, it's Dirk and about ten other people. It's two o'clock on Sunday fucking afternoon. We're standing outside your fucking rehearsal space in the cold. What happened? Where the fuck are you, man? We're hanging out for another half hour and then we're bolting. Hope to see you. Bye."

At 2:45, the rehearsal was officially called off. None of us had an apartment big enough to fit us all. We all started toward Times Square to catch our respective subways. We took our time about it. It was a beautiful, sunny Sunday afternoon, and it seemed like such a disappointment to part.

That's when we passed the bar. It wasn't one of those typical neighborhood bars with the wooden floors where the old guys showed up early in the morning to start drinking themselves to death. This one had stripes on the wall, an aquarium, and background Reggae music. It was designed and decorated for people like us. Someone suggested we go in for a couple of drinks. It didn't matter who said it because we were all thinking it at once.

The eleven of us sat around a large round table near the bar's large picture window, passing around a pitcher of blue Margaritas with tiny plastic fish and mermaids suspended in it. Then another. Then I stopped counting.

I looked out the window, nursing my big, sour drink with the salty rim. The sky was crisp and blue. A beautiful day to take a jog or walk around the reservoir at Central Park and watch the leaves turn, I mused.

I could remember the conversation only as little snippets: Dirk reading a recent review from *The Village Voice* by a lesbian reviewer who trashed the show but doted on Rose, and suggesting that if Rose put out, we might get better reviews. Angie recounting some pretentious fool in her acting class, telling the story of some doomed starlet who died overdosing on sleeping pills. Russell talking about the latest Sam Shepard play, how formulaic it was, and how easy it would be to write a Sam Shepard play. Spanky doing Brando in "Apocalypse Now," "On the Waterfront," and "Superman"; Gregory Peck as Atticus Finch in "To Kill a Mockingbird," making incestuous advances on Scout; and as the afternoon wore on and the ethanol haze enveloped us all, Popeye. We fancied ourselves the Algonquin Roundtable of the TV generation.

Hours later, when the sun had disappeared behind the tall buildings and the street was tinted blue, the bill came. Pat saw it first, and broke out laughing. "What is it, man?" Dirk asked, and when Pat handed it to him, he laughed too. When the bill wafted around to me, I saw the punch line: $342.43! More than my monthly rent.

I glanced at the door with fleeting thoughts of escape, but the waitress stood right in front of it, arms folded, amused yet cautious. Still laughing, we began throwing money down on the table. I threw down $60 because I knew about half of us couldn't afford dinner, let alone these silly pitchers of Margaritas. Over the next 15 minutes, we counted the pile and recounted, and people tossed dollars bills and, finally, quarters and dimes, onto the pile like campers throwing twigs on a campfire.

On the platform at West 4th, there was only one other passenger, a middle-aged black man way down at the end. After seeing me, he seemed happy to stay there. After several minutes, there was a faint breeze from the uptown direction–the earliest herald of an impending train, and I wandered to the edge of the platform for a look. Then I actually saw a light at the end of the tunnel. "D train, D train, D train," I chanted. Several minutes later, it was close enough to make out the letter B on the front of it. "Fuck!"

The black man boarded the train and it roared out of the

station. The platform never seemed so desolate as when a train had just left. For several minutes, all I heard was the humming of the lights overhead and the babbling of grimy little waterfalls from the gutters up above. Then there was a screech and some static over the loudspeaker, the tell-tale sign of an important message I was supposed to hear but couldn't.

After paying the bill at the bar, we splintered into smaller groups. Jim went off with Dirk to watch the Forty Niners game, leaving Angie a free agent. We decided to get something to eat at the White Horse. Very probably, I would wind up sleeping on the couch at her and Jim's apartment, as I often did after shows. The next morning, I would fetch them coffees and bagels, as I always did.

Angie phoned her sister Teresa, who was staying for a week with her and Jim, and told her to meet us at the White Horse. Then Angie and I cabbed it down to the White Horse. Since Jim and Angie were both currently out of work, I paid the fare.

The White Horse, only a few blocks from Jim and Angie's apartment, was a neat old bar with rough wood floors, an old fashioned brass bar, and a history: It was where Dylan Thomas had drunk himself to death one afternoon.

Angie waved to Teresa, who was sitting at a table in the back room, drinking coffee, and introduced us. Teresa was several years older than Angie and bore a strong family resemblance. I immediately found her to be a warm and engaging person, whose only fault in my eyes was that she wasn't quite Angie.

"What happened to Jim?" Teresa asked.

"He's with Dirk!" Angie snapped. "I'm getting so sick of him. Either he's off with Dirk, or Dirk's hanging around our apartment, or Jim's playing his stupid, fucking little Casio."

"I thought you bought him headphones for his birthday."

"I did. I thought it would be better if I didn't have to listen to his music all day, but this is worse. It's like I bought him a vibrator! I poke my head in and he's sitting there twiddling his little fingers and rocking his head back and forth in his stupid little Jim dreamworld! I can't stand it!"

When the waitress came, Angie and I ordered burgers and beers. Teresa ordered a salad and a club soda. I gave her a concerned look. "I can't drink," Teresa explained. "I'm a recovering alcoholic."

The look I gave her must have been suspicious and vaguely offended, because she put her hand on my shoulder and whispered, "Don't worry. I'm not here to baby-sit."

"See the crap I have to put up with Jim?" Angie said to me. "You should be happy you're unattached."

I mulled this one over and said, "Yeah, but I'd kind of like to have sex again before I die."

"You know what you should do? Write a play and produce it. I'm telling you, they'll all come out of the woodwork. All beautiful, all desperate. They'll be all over you like flies on shit!"

"Thanks," I said, for the simile, and added, "I've never written anything decent that's over ten minutes long."

"Who care about decent? These chicks just want to be in something, anything they can put on their resumes. I'm telling you, you'd have it made."

Our burgers, beers, salad, and club soda came, and we started right in. The ground beef came as a rude awakening to my stomach, which would have been just as happy to continue digesting liquids. I took several gulps of beer to wash down each bite, and then dabbed the napkin against my mustache to soak up the ketchup.

"Have you ever thought of shaving off your beard?" Angie suddenly asked.

"No, don't you like it?" She made a face and shook her head. "Why not?"

She stared at my face intently and I felt myself draw into

the gravity of her cold yet fiery dark eyes. "You can't tell what's going on behind it. It's like you're hiding something."

"Without it, I look fifteen."

"What's wrong with that? I like men who are still boys. I'd love to see what you look like without it."

"What's in it for me? What would you do if I shave it?"

"Anything you want."

"Anything?"

"Anything."

At that point, Teresa leaned over and spoke in my ear. "Before you do anything drastic, you should probably get it in writing."

A young policeman with a department-issue mustache came through the turnstile and looked up and down the platform. I could tell he was checking me out. After all, I looked like a drowned rat. He could probably tell I was drunk, but was trying to figure out if I was drunk enough to arrest or at least hassle. He walked back and forth behind me a couple of times the soles of his shoes clacking against the concrete and reverberating along the grimy tiles.

Soon another breeze came along and another train came roaring into the station. I cursed when I saw it was a B train. When the doors opened, the cop stuck his head in and looked around. Then he turned to me. "Where you headed?"

"Sheepshead Bay," I said in a tone that meant it was none of his business.

"You waiting for the D train?"

"Yeah, seeing as how that's the one that goes to Sheepshead Bay."

"Well, you could be waiting a long time. It's not running out of this station. Didn't you hear the announcement?"

"Fucking son of a bitch! What am I gonna do?"

"Take the B train to DeKalb and then switch over. The D's

running between DeKalb and the rest of Brooklyn."

I got on quickly and said, "Thanks, officer!"

He nodded almost imperceptibly, and then the doors closed, and I was finally bound for Brooklyn. A middle-aged Hispanic woman, the only other one on the car, looked at me nervously when I first got on, but when I sat down on the other end of the car and began to sob quietly, she relaxed.

Redundant though it may seem, Angie and I wanted to go out for after-dinner drinks. She called Dirk's apartment to discover Jim had left already. Then she called her answering machine and left Jim a message that we would be at Le Bistro.

Inside Le Bistro, we sat down at a cozy booth, with Angie and Teresa sitting across from me. The drizzle outside drummed lightly on the window next to our booth. The flickering candle at our table created shadows that enveloped us, gently ebbing and flowing. Angie and I each had red wines and Teresa had an apple-cinnamon herbal tea.

I reached into my pocket again to double check that I still had the paper napkin from the White Horse. On it, crudely written with the waitress's pen, was the contract: "I will do ANYTHING if Rob shaves his beard–Angie."

The coziness started to fade when the four troglodytes in the booth next to us took notice of the Angie and Teresa and began to whisper about them. If the four weren't actually brothers, their parents had apparently been swimming in the same scummy gene pool: All four of them had low foreheads, large cavernous brow ridges and the dim "I'm more cunning than you" expression one often sees in borderline-retarded prison convicts who think they're clever because they splashed someone's face with battery acid. I was pretty sure they were from New Jersey.

The four Bridge-and-Tunnel ambassadors did what their ilk was known for–encroaching and ruining what would have otherwise been a perfect scene. One of them, a slightly taller version of the other three who was probably the alpha male of the pack, asked, "Hey, we were wondering. You two sisters?"

"No, clones. Our dad was a genetic engineer," Teresa said, without missing a beat—or smiling.

"He wanted kids but our mom had her tubes tied," Angie said.

"We just figured you were related, you're both so hot-looking."

"Yeah, I'll bet every woman in the place looks good to you right about now," Angie said, yawning widely in their direction without even covering her mouth.

"What are your names?" one of them asked.

"That's strictly on a 'need to know' basis," Teresa snapped back.

Whether the area-code-201's were completely oblivious to the sarcasm or impervious to it, they carried on undeterred. Within just a few minutes, Teresa and Angie had surrendered their first names, and two of the hominids had infested our table. A few minutes later, one of them had sprouted an arm over Angie's shoulder. She neither encouraged nor rejected it, as long experience had taught her that either extreme would provoke him, but just kept the same bored expression on her face.

Angie reached into her purse, pulled out a pack of Merits, and probed it with her finger. It was empty. "Shit, I'm out!"

"You shouldn't smoke," said the Alpha Male sitting next to her.

"Is there a store near here?" Teresa asked.

"Just up the block," Angie said.

"I need some aspirin anyway. I'll get you some more Merits," Teresa said, and then turned to Alpha Male and barked "Move!"

He moved aside so she should get out, and Angie slid out of the seat as well. "A pretty girl like you shouldn't be walking alone at night," one of beta males said. "Let me escort you."

"I'll be fine."

"Can you get me a pack of Parliaments?" Alpha Male asked, but she was already halfway out the door and at least pretended not to hear. I latched onto Angie's arm and quietly guided her around to my side of the table. She slid in to the booth ahead of me, and I sat down on the outside, sealing her off.

Alpha Male suddenly realized that the game had changed. He didn't want to sit down opposite us, nor did he want to just stand there, looking like an idiot. He turned to his three subordinates and announced, "I'm going to the can."

Just then, something miraculous and unexpected happened. Something warm and wet probed into my ear canal. I turned my head and my lips collided with Angie's. Her mouth tasted hot and tangy, cured with cigarette smoke. I tried to take as much of her face as I could in my mouth, and could taste the salt of her cheek. But pretty soon it was my face being sucked into her mouth. I felt her tongue slide over my cheek and back into my ear. My whole body seemed to short circuit–if I weren't sedated, I would probably convulse–and she began to laugh teasingly. I immediately wanted to prove that I could be a deft and flamboyant lover, but in fact I was a helpless, quivering mass. She was toying with me sort of absentmindedly, much the way I'd seen cats catch mice, play with them, lick their coats affectionately as if they were kittens, and then let them go.

At that moment, I decided that life didn't have to be unrelentingly grim and drab. Life was full of wildly wonderful possibilities. Maybe there was a God.

I didn't know quite why it was happening. She could seduce virtually any man she met, and sexually she could take me or leave me. Maybe she wanted to get back at Jim. Maybe she wanted to do a number on the guys in the next booth. Or maybe she just knew how desperately I wanted her, had always wanted her, and had decided to ease my pain just a little.

I woke up near Coney Island with a full and insistent bladder. The subway car was empty and the doors were open. I got up and looked out the door to see the ghostly silhouettes of the tower and the Cyclone, long closed. I had slept past Sheepshead Bay, and there was no telling when the next train would be headed back toward Manhattan. I walked back to the Manhattan end of the train and looked in the motorman's compartment, but it was empty. The D train never completely shut down at night, but I knew the trains became less and less frequent.

Then there was the issue of my bladder. I didn't know if I could hold it till the train decided to head back and took its own sluggish time about it. And there was no bathroom in the station. I had once seen a bum awaken on a full subway train and empty himself sloppily into a half-empty bottle of Colt 45, and had vowed to never let myself sink that low.

The rain had ceased. I decided to walk it. It would take half an hour, but at least I was guaranteed of being home in half an hour and not be at the mercy of the whims of the subway system. I went down the steps and followed the elevated subway tracks back toward Manhattan. I found a nice hidden spot right under the tracks to urinate, but it wasn't really necessary. There wasn't a soul around anywhere.

It was isolated, it was dark, and it was very, very stupid for me to be walking here. Coney Island was known for junkies and gangs, and if I were attacked, there would be no one around to help. I walked briskly down the middle of the streets, until I reached Brighton Beach, where the boardwalk ended, and on to the foot bridge that traversed Sheepshead Bay. Usually the bridge was alive with fishermen, but tonight it was just me and the bridge.

After being lip-locked for about fifteen minutes, Angie and I slowly became aware of our surroundings again. Angie broke free first. "I wonder what happened to Teresa. She's been gone an awful long time," she said.

"Yeah, you better go out and look for her," someone said from the next booth, and I turned to see the four Garden State osteocephaloids grinning at us. "We'll take care of Angie while you're gone."

I didn't answer, but just gave him a pained expression, which he seemed to relish.

"I'll go look," said Angie.

"It's not safe. You could get raped or something," said Alpha Male. "If you go, we go with you."

"Let's both go look for her," I said to Angie.

"Yeah, but what if she comes back? You won't be here!" said Alpha Male.

"Then she'll know to meet us back at the apartment," Angie thought out loud.

"Your apartment? Where's that?" one of the beta males asked.

"Look, if she comes back, we'll tell her to meet you," said Alpha Male. "We'll tell her you two went to the Kit Kat Klub and she's supposed to meet you there. And, of course, we'll offer to drive her!"

I glared at Alpha Male, who seemed very, very pleased with himself. I had no doubt he would do what he said he'd do, and worse.

"You better go," said one of the guys. "She mighta been mugged. She mighta been hit by a car. She might be lying in the gutter bleeding somewhere."

"Shut the fuck up!" Angie cried out.

"You kiss your mother with that mouth?"

In another very uncomfortable 20 minutes, Teresa came bursting into the room, out of breath.

"Teresa, where have you been?" Angie asked.

"With Jim. I found him wandering back toward Perry

Street, crying. He said he came in and saw you two making out. We've been in the apartment, talking. He's really upset."

The guys in the next booth were slapping the table and laughing now. This was apparently even better than Saturday night wrestling.

"I think I've calmed him down a little. He's ready to see you, and he definitely doesn't want to see Rob."

Angie grabbed her temples as if reacting to a sudden shriek. "Shit! Shit! Shit!" she said, and turned to me, "This is what we'll tell him. We'll tell him I was drunk and tried to seduce you and you tried to fight me off."

"He's not going to believe that, is he?"

"He's got to."

The three of us left Le Bistro together, thankfully without the New Jersey Neanderthals, and took the long short walk to Jim and Angie's apartment.

From the footbridge at Sheepshead Bay, I walked several blocks to Shore Drive, which abutted my apartment building. A hundred yards to my left, cars continued to swish by on the Expressway, but Shore Drive was completely dead. I jogged past two blocks of identical brick apartment buildings until I came to mine.

I fumbled the key in the lock and ran up the stairs to my studio. I fumbled another key in another lock and retreated to the familiarity of my studio apartment–to my bed, to my desk and typewriter, to my TV perched on the dining-room chair, to my stereo sitting on the floor, and to my kitchen/dining room table, where my answering machine sat blinking with a message.

Quickly, I began peeling off my wet clothes, which clung like a new layer of skin. Once I'd gotten them off and thrown them into the bathtub, I climbed into some gym shorts and a T-shirt. I glanced in the mirror to see that my wet hair was so matted to the side of my head that bald streaks showed through. Next, I went to the refrigerator, located in the tiny alcove that was my kitchen, grabbed an ice-cold Becks, popped the cap, and sat down in front of the answer machine. I took a gulp and then pressed the playback button.

"*Hi, honey. It's Angie,*" came her boozy, breathy voice. "*I hope you're okay. I'm just calling to see if you're okay. And to say it's okay. Don't worry, honey. Everything's going to be okay. And I love you. And I just hope you're okay. Okay? Okay, bye.*"

I played the message three more times and went to bed.

ROB DINSMOOR

MASTER OF SEDUCTION

I would have gone to one of Jim and Angie's parties anyway, but on top of everything else, I was supposed to meet Uma.

"She's a really pretty girl in my acting class, from Sweden. I think you'd like her," said Angie and then asked Jim "Don't you think he'd like Uma?"

"I don't know. I have to be honest with you, Rob, she's a little... how shall we say it... hefty," Jim said. Angie slapped him on the back of the head. "Honey, lamb chop, love of my life, why do you always hurt me so?" he laughed.

Still I was curious. If nothing else, I wanted to know: How many people could they fit in that tiny apartment of theirs? The tiny ten-by-ten living room, with a couch and arm chair they rescued from the street, looked out over a charming courtyard in the back. In the bedroom, the bed was suspended six feet above the floor and had only two feet of head space. Underneath it, several yards of clothes hung, most of them Angie's, and below that, the extensive shoe collection Angie had garnered as a shoe model. The toilet, an old-fashioned model with a pull chain, was in a closet at the end of the bedroom, with old-West-style swinging doors. Between the two rooms was the tiny kitchen, in the middle of which was the bathtub, with a discreet curtain around it for privacy. I had always felt at home in that apartment.

I was already in a very happy mood by the time I showed up at their apartment. It was the middle of summer, the night air was warm and inviting, and doors and windows all over Manhattan were open. I had wandered by the White Horse to hear a muted but excited roar coming through its open doorway, and had happened upon a recently vacated barstool. I loved that bar but rarely spoke to anyone in it. I just let several conversations waft over me at once, watched the bartender bounce around, making drinks, and listened to the constant roar of ice trays being dumped. Life was good.

When I stepped out three beers later, the pores in the back of my nose had relaxed and there was even more excitement in the air. In a single warm, moist breath, I inhaled traces of sour keg beer, perfume, cigarette smoke, tar, baked sidewalk, the Hudson River just three blocks away, and stir-fried garlic from the Chinese restaurant across the street. My olfactory lobe was active, my body was on autopilot, and my id was free to roam. Somewhere deep within me, the Master had awakened, and he was hungry for love.

After buying beer at the Italian deli, I entered Jim and Angie's walk-up. I could hear the party going from the first floor. At the fourth floor of the walk-up, I encountered a wall of people hanging out by the railing: Amid the throng of tossed back hair, halter tops, and wafting skirts were Gretchen, the thin, bratty German waitress from Jim's restaurant; Jim's pleasant sister Judy; Rose's cute but overly made-up tall-haired friend Rhonda with the shrill voice. With so many women in one place, my male radar was working overtime: Yes, no, maybe, too old, too fat, bad posture, jaw too big, striking features but maybe too androgynous. As I came around the railing to go into Jim and Angie's apartment, I saw a pair of glistening tan legs in cut-offs butterflied in an arm chair in the apartment next door. Oh, definitely, yes.

I glided into their apartment, slowly square-danced between the warm bodies I encountered on my way to the kitchen, shook hands with the host, kissed the hostess on the cheek, put the six pack in the fridge, and opened one of the bottles. With a lit cigarette perched in her hand, Angie spun me around 180 degrees from the counter, asked me if I'd met her friend Uma, which of course I hadn't, and proceeded to introduce her and her friend Cissi.

Angie capped off my introduction by mentioning that I ran five miles a day, an introduction I savored as I commandeered Angie's cigarette, inhaled half an inch of it, blew the smoke upward into a giant plume that lingered ominously by the ceiling. And then handed it back to her.

I immediately sized up Uma, with her chunky frame but cute face and an assertive smile to compensate for her heftiness, who had pressed just a few pounds per square inch too hard when applying lipstick to her supple lips. Cissi, a mousy, scholarly-looking blonde, squinted at me through her John Lennon glasses, lips slightly parted–an expression I interpreted as a mixture of shock and disapproval. I vowed then to make about five minutes of polite conversation and bolt.

As expected, the first thing out of Uma's mouth, albeit with an adorable lilt, was a comment about how awkwardly I held Angie's cigarette and how it just didn't suit me, but I'd heard it all before from hefty but assertive girls and the maternal thing just left me so cold.

It was nice meeting you, I've heard such nice things about you, I said, by way of an exit line. I made my way toward the tan legs in the cut-offs in the arm chair in the apartment next door, but when I got there the armchair was vacant and there was no sign of tan legs or cut-offs anywhere.

As I looked around, I overheard a conversation on one of my favorite subjects, mental illness. A striking woman in her mid forties with kinky auburn hair and long red fingernails was telling Rhonda about her bout with postpartum depression, and Rhonda shrieked, "What's that?"

Stepping right into the conversation, I explained that postpartum depression was mental depression precipitated by childbirth, probably due to a hormonal etiology but also the overwhelming realization that one has another life to be responsible for. Both women stared at me and then the red fingernail lady asked me how the hell I knew so much about it. I explained I was a medical writer and was well versed in all issues related to the human body, and then gave her this little head-to-toe look.

How was it treated? I asked. Was it a selective serotonin reuptake inhibitor? But she explained that they had treated her with tricyclic antidepressants.

How unfortunate for you, I said. I explained to Rhonda how serotonin reuptake inhibitors worked, how they were a boon to the treatment of depression and that all too often, in the past, hapless depressed patients were treated with electroconvulsive shock therapy, which caused memory loss and was absolutely barbaric. At this point, I looked around the room to see that virtually everyone in the room—including Uma, Cissi, Jim, and Angie, who had just stepped into the room, and the pixieish tanned-legged girl in the cut-offs, who was back to her rightful place on the armchair—were intently focused on our conversation.

"Electroshock worked for me," the red-fingernail lady responded. "It was the only thing that was able to bring me out of it."

Now it was my turn to raise an eyebrow and I looked at her for signs of irony, but she was dead serious. No short-term memory loss? I asked and she responded, none whatsoever. And it wasn't like in "Cuckoo's Nest," she explained, where the convulsions are violent and painful. It was more like being anesthetized.

Despite her bold refuting of my earlier statement, she was locked in, and so was everyone else. We swapped stories about favorite psychotropic and non-psychotropic medications and I waxed poetic on the effects of booze, cigarettes, marijuana, LSD and sex on neurotransmitters. I explained the effects of the menstrual period on appetite, the link between neurotransmitters and sexual deviance, the psychophysiology behind auto-erotic asphyxiation, why dope gives us the munchies, why men's stomachs growl after sex, and why hangovers sometimes leave people feeling inexplicably horny.

The fact that I was obviously making most of it up didn't seem to matter much. People were eating it up like a scary camp-fire story. By now, I realized I was on a very weird tack, but my sails were rustling, my bow was cutting deep, and my centerboard was just humming. The whole time, I kept my eye on the tan-legged girl. I caught her eye and she smiled at me.

Suddenly, the red-nailed lady clasped my jaw in her hand, her red nails digging ever so slightly into my left cheek, and whispered in my ear: "Listen very carefully, Romeo. My daughter's only fifteen, and anything that might happen between you two could result in jail time or death."

"Your daughter? Who's your daughter?"

"That young lady whose crotch you've been staring at for the last ten minutes," she responded. I glanced up briefly at Miss Tan Legs again, and saw that she now looked concerned and had her knees up in front of her chest in the fetal position. "You seem like a bright fellow but not very observant, so let me give you some advice. If I were you, I'd focus my attention on that little blonde Swedish number by the door. She hasn't taken her eyes off you since you came in here."

I glanced over at Uma's friend Cissi, her lips still parted, her glasses somewhat fogged over. She took them off, and cliché though it may be, without them, she was beautiful. She now looked quintessentially Swedish, like one of the singers in Abba or some sexy but naïve foreign exchange student in one of the beach party movies from the sixties. And I now realized that expression wasn't disapproval—in fact, it was the furthest thing from it.

• • •

I awoke on the floor to the sound of the phone ringing with the taste of brine and baby oil in my mouth. Cissi, totally naked, sat up from the couch and draped the sheet over her breasts. After a few rings, Angie came into the room to pick up the phone. "Hello," she said, and as she talked on the phone, I realized it was probably Dirk setting up the next rehearsal. "Wednesday's no good for me," she said, her expression blank, and her eyes began to wander around the room. They lit briefly on Cissi, who was still trying to focus her eyes and grabbing her T-shirt, and then on me, her eyes widening slightly and then rolling. Then she turned and stared out the window, as if something in the courtyard had caught her eye, during which time Cissi finished dressing and I slipped back into my jeans.

Last night, the party had thinned down to just the five of us. Uma fell asleep on Jim and Angie's loft bed, much to Jim's chagrin. I chivalrously offered to take the floor of the living room so Cissi could take the couch. Exactly what happened after that, I really couldn't say. Only the Master knew.

BAD KARMA

I awoke from my cat nap when my train pulled into West 4th. I had one bag wedged behind my legs and had the strap of another one wrapped around my right wrist so that neither of them would quietly walk away while I was sleeping. The doors opened and I saw it—an N train idling across the platform. Sweet Jesus! A miracle! An N train, no waiting.

I hoisted my bag and rushed across the platform onto the N. Then a horrible realization hit me. I turned and saw my other bag still sitting next to my seat on the D train.

I rushed back across the platform just as the doors to the D train were closing. I wedged my hand in between the closing doors and tried in vain to open them again. The engine revved up again and I yanked my wedged hand from the doors rather than risk being dragged, as sometimes happened to commuters, with tragic results.

As the train pulled out of the station, I briefly considered trying to jump on between the cars, but it just wasn't quite worth it. I had made an awful mistake, but I didn't deserve to die for it.

I had the bag with my VCR, but the bag with all of the videos for the show that night was on its way to the Bronx.

"Whassup?" called the conducter from the N train.

"My bag is still on the D train! I've got to get it! How can I get it?" The conductor just stared at me, silently. "Can you radio ahead or something?"

"No can do," he said. "You could catch the next train to the Bronx. Chances are they'll see it at the end of the line and bring it to the station's lost and found."

I found a pay phone, fished a quarter out of my pocket to feed it, waited for the N train to pull out of the station, and dialed the number for work. I was relieved that it was Grace, not Anna, who answered, "Biomedical Communications."

Grace and I had a nice rapport. She made manuscripts look beautiful when she typed them. "Grace, it's Rob."

"Hi, Rob."

"Is the Trilateral Commission in yet?"

"Jim and Maryanne are out, probably won't be in for another hour, but Richard's here, in his office, with the door closed."

"Grace, could you do me a favor? Could you just relay this message for me? When Jim gets in, tell him I'm as sick as a dog, I've been projectile vomiting since dawn, probably from some bad sushi, so I don't know if and when I'll be coming in."

Just then, another D Train roared deafeningly into the station. As it decrescendoed into a low roar, I could just barely make out Grace asking, "Just where are you, anyway?"

"You don't want to know."

"I'll give him the message. Is everything okay, Rob?"

"Not great, but thanks for asking. If I don't see you today, have a great weekend."

"Thanks. You too."

An hour and a half later, I was riding the elevator to my office, holding my one bag. The trip to the terminal station in The Bronx had been a complete bust. As I burst into the office, I announced, "Hi, Grace! Hi, Anna! All better! Any messages?"

"Yeah, three," Anna said in a chastising voice.

"Thanks," I said, grabbing them. As I walked to my office, I quickly looked at them. The typesetter. My mother. The Chief of Endocrinology at the Albert Einstein College of Medicine in the Bronx, with corrections to his manuscript. They would all have to wait. When I got into my private office, which overlooked the dreary landscape of abandoned factories of Long Island City, I shut the door and locked it.

I took a deep breath and dialed Dirk's number. When he answered, I just blurted it out, "Dirk, it's Rob. I lost the show tapes."

For 15 seconds, there was complete silence. "How did it happen?"

"I fell asleep on the subway and when I switched trains, I left the bag."

"Well, I hope you're well rested now. I hope you feel fan-fucking-tastic!"

"I feel terrible! But, look, Paul keeps all the masters. And he's got tapes from other shows. Maybe we can use some of the videos from past shows, mix and match, reconstruct the show's order."

"I'll call Paul up. You better hope he can do it. You'll be hearing from me."

An hour later, I was taking changes over the phone from the Chief of Endocrinology at Albert Einstein College of Medicine. "On galley three, line sixteen, instead of 'blood glucose elevation,' I want to say 'glycemic excursion.' That sounds a little sexier, don't you think?" A rap came on the door.

"Go away!" I shouted, cupping the mouthpiece.

"It's Grace. Your friend Dirk is on line one."

"Thanks, Grace!"

My mind raced, trying to come up with any conceivable reason for putting the Chief of Endocrinology at Albert Einstein College of Medicine on hold. Fortunately, since I had ever lied to him before, he trusted me. "Dr. Hauptmann? Listen, I have to go. They're evacuating the building. Some kind of fire drill or some-thing. I'll call you Monday."

"Holy shit, Rob. Get out of there. I've been to your build-ing—it's a death trap!"

I pressed line one. "Listen very carefully," Dirk said evenly, like a kidnapper making ransom demands. "Paul is taking half a day off from work to see if he can reconstruct the fucking video line-up you lost. He's going to get to the West Bank by four. You need to be there when he gets there. You're going to need to cue up all the tapes. And guess what? Some of the videos are on the same tape, and not in the proper order. Sound complicated? You bet your fucking life."

At 3:15, I came out of my office in my coat, carrying the VCR bag. My boss, Jim, was hanging out in the reception area, drinking coffee and dictating to Grace, who was starting to nod off, as she always did when Jim gave her dictation. "Jeeze, you look awful!" he said, with a mixture of amusement and concern.

He was right. The show loomed over me like a thunder-cloud. I hadn't had breakfast or lunch, only coffee, because my digestive tract was on the fritz. My stomach burned, I belched constantly and, in the privacy of my office, I had had a full-fledged anxiety attack, with trembling and tingling I thought would make my arms snap off. "I'm sorry," I rasped. "I feel like shit. I really shouldn't have come in. I'm going home."

"Sounds like a good idea. Get some sleep," Jim said. I knew he didn't want to catch whatever it was I had.

As I stepped out the door, Grace whispered, "Break a leg."

I took the subway to the Times Square station and walked toward the West Bank Café. When I was half a block away, I saw Rick and Spanky getting out of a cab with two full garbage bags of costumes and props, getting a television set out of the trunk, and waiting by the curb for others to show up. Had I not known them, I would have assumed that they had just burglarized someone's apartment. They noticed me just as I was crossing the street to the West Bank. I mimed jumping in front of a cab, and they applauded, but they weren't smiling.

I carried the VCR into the basement, where the theatre space was, and on my way back up, I encountered Rick and

Spanky, neither of whom looked at me or spoke to me. Back out on the street, Pat was guarding the TV, looking really annoyed. "They asked me to guard the TV, and then took off," Pat kvetched. Then he gestured toward the TV set expectantly. Maybe taking on the role of TV mover would restore some of the karma. We lifted it and began carrying it through the café.

"I guess I'm fucked," I said.

"Well, let's put it this way. You're lucky you live in Twentieth Century America. Because if you lived in Eighteenth Century Japan, you'd have only one course of action open to you." That was all Pat had to say on the subject.

After Pat and I had gotten the TV up onto its stand and plugged it in, Dirk showed up with his own garbage bag full of costumes and props. He paused long enough to shove a photocopied sheet in my face. "Here's the new show order," he said.

I immediately set to work laying out the fifty-foot coaxial cable I'd brought along with the tape deck. I attached one end to the tape deck, threaded it along the wall, and attached the other end to the TV. Then I used my roll of duct tape to affix the whole cable to the floor, so that some audience member wouldn't trip on it, break his neck, and send the TV hurtling off its six-foot stand onto the head of some other audience member. Paul showed up with a backpack full of videos and stacked them on one of the tables next to my video deck. I looked him in the eyes. There was no malice in them. "You know, in a way, I'm glad this happened," he said. "I've been telling Dirk for months that we have to do the videos differently. He's got to give me the order of the videos at least a few days in advance. That way I can dub a special tape just for that show, and you only have to deal with one tape instead of ten. I knew something like this would happen some day. Maybe now he'll listen."

Then he gave me one of his trademark clenched smiles, as if he were bracing for some kind of collision. "Here are the tapes

ROB DINSMOOR

for tonight's show. 'A Doll's House,' 'Mary Lou Retton's Cooking for the Gold Video,' 'Pinstripe Plaza' are all cued. As you can see from the new order, we're substituting 'English Conversation' for "Man-Woman.' It's cued, too. Now, here's where it gets tricky. 'The Droopy Zone,' 'The Naked Postal Zone,' and 'Chucklehead Multiplex' are all on the same tape. 'Droopy Zone' comes first in the show, but is second on the tape. 'Naked Postal Zone' comes second in the show but first on the tape. 'Chucklehead Multiplex' is last both on the tape and in the show. And of course there are a few scattered segments in between the three of them. So, what you've got to do is play 'Droopy Zone,' and then, using the tape counter, rewind to exactly where 'Naked Postal Zone' starts. Once 'Naked Postal Zone' is over, fast forward exactly to the beginning of 'Chucklehead Multiplex.' I've marked the time count for all of the segments right on the tapes themselves, but you'll have to do some quick math in your head. Got it?"

I almost threw up then and there.

How had I sunk so low in life? If I had gone to medical school when I graduated college, I would be a bonafide doctor by now. At least then, I would get some respect. Maybe it wasn't too late: I could take a few chemistry and biology classes at Brooklyn College, and maybe get into someplace like the University of Guadeloupe.

Once upon a time, half the skits in the show were mine, but now I was lucky to get one or two in. Early in the troupe's history, I had volunteered to get off the stage and help with the techie stuff—a decision I would regret for the rest of my life.

I hated it. I wasn't cut out for it. I had never been quick on my feet, and no amount of beer ever seemed to be able to squelch the abject terror I felt when the lights went down and all the opportunities to fuck up presented themselves. And for putting up with that terror night after night, the only thanks I got was attitude and ostracism.

Peter showed up and began running the lighting cues with Dirk. He had an elegant and elaborate system worked out on a sheet of paper that he taped up next to the light booth. As he masterfully manipulated the 10 control knobs, occasionally taking note of Dirk's corrections and patiently addressing them, he had this benign, zen smile on his face. One sensed that he loved every aspect of this job and there was nowhere he'd rather be. God how I hated that smug sonofabitch.

Judy, another one of the writer/techie/whores, showed up with the programs. "I'm really excited," I overheard her say to Angie. "Jami Bernard from the *Post* is coming—she always gives us good ink—and Bill Irvilino from the *Village Voice* said he was hoping to show up, too."

At 7:40, they still weren't yet serving drinks downstairs, so I went upstairs to the bar to get myself a couple of beers. As I came to the top of the stairs, there were already about 20 people in line to see the show, a far bigger crowd than usually showed up this early. One of them was Erika, my former boss, who had always said, "One of these days, I really want to see your show," but never did—until now. Why tonight?

I smiled, waved, and disappeared behind the bar, where I got myself two bottles of Rolling Rock to get the night rolling. I waved to Erika again as I hurried back down the stairs, downing half of one of the bottles in one gulp.

The "door" opened 5 minutes later, and the stampede began. The place almost immediately filled up, except for the two tables with the "Reserved" placards set aside for the theater reviewers. And they kept coming. Frantically, the Yale Mafia that managed the West Bank went into action, bringing extra tables and chairs from the back rooms and scooting the original tables closer together. Mindy (Yale School of Drama '85) dashed around frantically taking drink orders. Lewis Black, the West Bank's artistic director, eyed the table my videocorder was sitting on, but I threw myself on top of it, shaking my head.

There were 60, maybe 70 people packed in that little room. I had never seen an audience so big.

Dirk came out, whispered in Peter's ear, and quickly darted back behind the curtain. I knew he was giving Peter the go-ahead. Here we go. Fasten your seat belts. No turning back now. The rollercoaster ride has begun. Peter dimmed the house lights. Lewis Black came on stage. Peter put the spot on him.

"Hello, I'm Lewis Black and I'm the artistic director and playwright-in-residence here at the West Bank. You wouldn't believe what kind of doors that opens for me," he began bitterly, and I could tell he was going into his usual spiel. He delivered his introduction while smoking a cigarette, holding it between his thumb and first two fingers, like a cross between Rod Serling and Humphrey Bogart, but with long, curly hair and glasses. "Here at the West Bank, we're devoted to giving you intelligent entertainment, two words you usually don't hear in the same sentence. Each week, we premier one-act plays by some of the most talented new playwrights in New York." He took a drag of his cigarette and surveyed the quiet audience warily.

"That's usually the reaction I get—stunned silence. 'I don't get it!' you're thinking. 'Why would anyone want to do something like that?' Because good playwrights cut their teeth writing one-act plays performed in dingy, depressing little basements like this one.

"Before I introduce tonight's act, I want to remind you that New York yuppies are the first people since the reign of the Sun King who think that other people were born to serve them. So, please remember the folks serving you. Tip them generously. Theirs is a thankless, horrible job.

"The ensemble you are about to see performs some of the best sketch comedy you'll see in this city. And they are an ensemble in every sense of the word, working together with this bizarre synergy that is just, well, sick. Ladies and gentlemen, you're in for a treat. Put your hands together for Chucklehead."

Applause. The spot went down and Lewis Black left the front of the stage. The curtain was pulled open to a dark stage.

I crossed my fingers and pressed the "Play" button. The video came up. It was Spanky, playing some sort of postapocalyptic survivor in rags, running away from he camera in the rubble of bombed-out buildings (actually just a fairly typical block in Alphabet City, taped on our "hit-and-run" video expeditions). The cameraman catches up to him and asks him about life before the war. The survivor doesn't remember much, except for this group of comedians called Knucklehead. Chucklehead. "Ten of them, and eight feet tall they was."

"Were they funny?"

"No!"

"Do you remember anything about them?" At this question, the survivor looks off in contemplation, the video fades out.

I pressed "Stop" and "Eject" and fumbled the tape out of its slot. The laughter and applause reached a crescendo and started to fade. Before it died completely, the lights come up on the first sketch, all set up with everyone in place. It was Peter's "Noisy Apartment," and the audience timidly began to laugh. A good sign. We had tamed them. I double-checked the show order and inserted "A Doll's House" into the video deck. Confident that the show was crackling, things were prepared, and the sketch had at least a couple more minutes left in it, I treated myself to the luxury of gulping half my bottle of beer and retreated to a warm and cozy chamber of my brain.

Forty-five minutes later, things were just sailing along. At first, the audience had poked at our comedy politely with their knives and forks. Then they began shoveling in the belly laughs with both hands. Now they were all face down in the same messy trough, lapping up all the gags, no matter how sour, bitter, or tainted they tasted. Even my usually timid ex-boss Erika was laughing with demonic glee.

While focusing on tasks at hand, I was still able to order two more beers from Mindy and even race upstairs for a pit stop during one of the longer skits.

I was gratified by the way "Up with Smoke" totally surprised the audience, like a herd of deer caught in the headlights of a rapidly approaching Mack truck. They knew something big and wicked was coming, but couldn't tell exactly what.

It was my idea and my original script, but the final production was an ensemble effort. A saccharin pre-school teacher (Rose) introduces "Up with Smoke" and its moderator, Jack Winston from the R.J. Morris Tobacco Institute (Dirk). He talks about important decisions about things like what grammar school you plan to attend or whether to make smoking a part of your personal lifestyle. He introduces the prestigious winner of the Tobacco Institute's Playwriting Prize, in which Thomas Jefferson (Rick) stands up for his smoking rights. A crippled construction worker with a gravelly voice (Spanky), his neck in a neck brace and a cigarette sticking out of the corner of his mouth, describes how not standing up for his smoking rights ruined his life–he was asked to step outside from a construction site ten floors up. An adorable smoking dog puppet named Puff McDuff (the voice of Rose) visits Dr. Puppet (also the voice of Rose) complaining of nervousness, and Dr. Puppet tells him it's because he quit smoking–and laughs at the notion that cigarettes are harmful.

When Puff McDuff and the rest of the characters launched into Jim's bouncy little song about Puff being arrested for smoking a cigarette in a restaurant, the audience went nuts. They continued laughing at the end of the song, as the members of the troupe began tossing loose cigarettes into the audience.

Throughout the skit, half of my attention was focused on The Big Switch. I took out the videotape that was in the deck and replaced it with the one that had shown "The Naked Postal Zone" about 15 minutes earlier. The tape counter now showed "21:35." The segment after "The Naked Postal Zone" started—on that tape—at 11:16. Figuring that there were three seconds between segments, that tape was now up to 11:13. "Chucklehead Multiplex" started at 15:07. That meant I had to fast forward 3 minutes and 54 seconds. Twenty-one minutes and 35 seconds plus 3 minutes and 54 seconds came to . . . 25 minutes and 29 seconds. Didn't it?

I fast forwarded and tried to stop it at exactly at 25:29 but it stopped at 25:26. A couple of seconds extra wouldn't hurt, would it? Unless the tape wound up showing a little bit of the previous segment. A little shaky but not the end of the world. The lights came down on "Up with Smoke." After the laughter had peaked, I pressed "Play." For several seconds, there was complete darkness on the screen.

Then, miraculously, the "Chucklehead Multiplex" video came up. I wanted to raise my fist and fill the room with a whooping war cry. Instead, I did a quiet little victory dance in my tiny little corner of the room. Being the class arithmetic champ in third grade had finally paid off.

Next, I put the audio tape into the audio tape player for Russell's "About Men Rap," coming up right after "Chucklehead Multiplex." It was one of the perennial showpieces satirizing the self-indulgent male crybaby stories in the "About Men" column of the *New York Times Magazine*. The tape provided the base beat for the rap that Angie, Dirk, Spanky, and Pat recited and break-danced to. They had performed it easily 50 times and knew every beat by heart. Carefully, I pushed "Pause" and then "Play" so that when I pressed "Pause" again, the tape would start instantly.

As the video faded to black, I pressed "Stop." I could switch tapes later—right now, I had to be vigilant so as to time the tape for "About Men" just right.

Lights up on Angie, dressed in a revealing nightie, holding

the Sunday *New York Times*. She proceeded to talk about her favorite section, the "About Men" column. "Because I am learning so much . . . "

"ABOUT MEN!" chanted Dirk, Pat, and Spanky, coming on stage in business suits and shades. "G-E-E-E-T *FRESH!*" At the end of "Get," I pressed the pause button, so that the first beat (wump!) would be simultaneous with the word "fresh." "Wump! Wump! Wump! Tatatatat!" Except this time the tape started on "Tatatatat."

Spanky rushed into his verse, trying to catch up to the tape. Dirk and Pat were marching to the beats of entirely different drummers. "Stop the tape!" Peter whispered loudly to me from the lighting booth. "Rewind!"

I waved him off. The first rule of the theater, taught to me by my high school drama coach, is never to admit you've fucked up. Just go with the flow and wing it. That's professionalism.

"I left–wife cold–for–lady–and bold. I know it's–rotten–but–don't do it often," said Spanky, now skipping entire words in his mad dash to catch up. Pat and Dirk, dancing side by side, were now flailing their arms and legs wildly like Siamese twins sharing an epileptic fit.

"Stop the tape!" Peter implored again. "Stop the tape!"

"STOP THE FUCKING TAPE!" Spanky thundered over the on-stage mike. I pressed "Stop." "NOW REWIND!"

I rewound the tape, watched the counter return to zero.

"Ladies and Gentlemen, I want you to give a round of applause to our audiovisual expert Rob, who apparently had one sixpack too many before the show," Dirk said, motioning toward me. There were a couple of lone claps before the audience realized it was sarcasm.

"NOW YOU GET TO HEAR THE SONG THE WAY IT'S SUPPOSED TO BE!" Spanky announced.

"It's at the beginning of the tape!" I called. "It's not cued!"

"JUST PLAY THE FUCKING THING!"

I pressed "Play." Several seconds of silence ensued. Then, "Wump! Wump! Wump! Ratatatatat!" And so on. And the four performers stuck to the beat flawlessly. The audience applauded as the lights went down. The rest of the show went seamlessly. The audience applauded and even stood. Pat introduced each of the performers, as well as Peter and me, without any gratuitous editorializing.

The house lights came up. I sat in my corner, reasonably hidden from view, and they started gathering up cables, packing my bag, and hoisting TVs.

After fulfilling my post-show responsibilities, I quickly headed over to the Blarney Rock, our post-show hangout. I parked the VCR under one of the long tables in back and immediately went to the bar to order the night's first communal pitcher of beer. Next to where I stood, a lean, muscular young man about my age sat half-collapsed over a tall mug of beer, a glistening thread of spittle suspended between his lips and the mug. I was surprised the bartender was still serving him. He turned to me, put his hand on my shoulder, and slurred a number of syllables at me, ending with "amigo."

"How ya doin'?" I said as pleasantly as I could.

"Ayyyyyight," he said, smiling sentimentally, and then nodded off, giving me the opportunity to escape with the pitcher.

I brought the pitcher over to my table, returned with a number of glasses, and sat down. The troupe came filing in. They were all engrossed in conversation, mostly about who butchered what line and who borrowed whose wig during the show and didn't return it. None of them spoke to me. As people milled around, the glasses and some of the beer in the pitcher disappeared, but no one sat down at the table. No one spoke to me and frankly I couldn't think of anything I really wanted to say to these people.

My muscular drunk amigo was slowly making his way

back toward me and not having an easy time of it. He moved in short bursts, steadying himself on the back of someone's chair, then the end of the bar, then on one of the supporting columns, and then on the end of my table. He reached into his pocket, pulled out a quarter, and held it out to me.

"Well thank you!" I said, much the way I would speak to a grandmother with Alzheimer's. "What's this for?"

He looked around the room, trying to get his bearings, and then pointed to the jukebox. "Oh, you want me to put the quarter into the juke box?" I asked. He nodded. "Is there anything in particular you want to hear?" He shook his head.

I went to the jukebox, put the quarter in, and punched up, "Pink Cadillac." It was an old favorite of the troupe's. When I came back to my table, the guy was already on his way back to his bar stool.

I grabbed my coat and video deck and began my long journey back to Brooklyn.

A NIGHT TO FORGET

I got off the N Train at the Broadway stop in Astoria. I clutched the railing going down the steps, but once I was on the street, I was on my own–and the street was shifting back and forth.

Things shifted clockwise, causing the sidewalk on my left to rear up and forcing me to push off with my right leg just to stay more or less vertical, and then counterclockwise, forcing me to push off with my left leg. I accelerated this gait into a sort of serpentine jog, hoping to make it back to our apartment while I was still, more or less, vertical. Fortunately, here and there, I found a telephone pole or a hydrant or a parked car to hold onto when the tilting became too intense.

I looked down. The knees of my suit were filthy. Apparently, I'd fallen at some point that night.

I stumbled past two Greek restaurant/pizza parlors, the deli, Walken's Bakery (once owned by Christopher Walken's family), and the neighborhood tavern. Fortunately, there was no one out on the street to witness this sad spectacle. Or, if there were, I was lucky enough not to notice them.

I turned a corner to the left, then to the right, then to the left again, and I was on 28th Street. Now I ran alongside the apartment buildings, occasionally pushing off with my right hand when one of the buildings threatened to come crashing down on me. Finally, I came to my door.

I looked quickly around. A friend of mine who lived only two blocks down from here had been brutally mugged while trying to get into his apartment building, and he wasn't even drunk. Two guys came at him and one hit him in the forehead with the butt of a rifle or shotgun. Blood gushed everywhere and got matted into his hair. They had to shave the top of his head just to get in all the stitches and he looked hideous, but he felt he'd come out ahead because they never got his wallet.

I tilted forward and propped my head against the door as I fumbled the keys out of my pocket. I tried sticking several of them into the lock at various angles until it dawned on me that the outer door didn't even have a lock. I turned the doorknob and went flying into the lobby. I hit my head against the inner door, rubbed my head to check for blood, and leaned against that door as I found the right key.

The three flights of stairs slanted upward at a 75 degree angle, sometimes forcing me to go on all fours. As I crawled up the stairs, I looked at my watch: 10:15. I found myself wishing it were much later.

When I got to my apartment, I started fumbling the keys into the lock, until the door magically flew open. I entered just in time to see Kari's back as she disappeared down the corridor and into the kitchen. Was she pissed at me? It was too early to tell. But first things first. I went into the bathroom, unzipped my fly, and siphoned what seemed like gallons of fluid from my bladder.

When I came into the kitchen, I found Kari at the kitchen table, smoking a cigarette and laying out tarot cards. From my angry adolescent days studying demonology, I recognized the pattern: It was the ancient Celtic method with a cross and a scepter. "Doin' a tarot reading?" I asked.

"That's right," she said flatly, not looking up.

"Some personal quession you wan' answered? Some big life quession?"

"Something like that."

Even in my inebriated state, I was pretty sure what the question was. "Well, I'm gonna bed," I said.

"That's probably a wise decision."

I went into the bedroom, took off most of my clothes, and fell into bed. When I awoke, I was in bed alone with a hangover of epic proportions. "Kari?" I called out. There was no answer. I wandered around the apartment, but there was no sign of her–just her cat Ouzo, who looked up, startled, from licking himself as I poked my head in the living room. Would she have moved back to Boston without him?

The night before, I had thrown my suit over a chair. I picked it up and began emptying the pockets. From the inside pocket of my jacket, I pulled out a photograph. It was of me standing in front of a bar with rosy cheeks, a crooked smile, and a parrot on my shoulder. Had there been a parakeet at Peter's bachelor party? No, the parrot was earlier. Much, much earlier . . .

It was the night of Peter's bachelor party, which was supposed to start at 7:30 p.m. Given that it was Peter and that both men and women were invited, I expected it to be pretty tame. I was supposed to meet Rick at 7:00 and go over with him. At 4:30, I was meeting with a client in midtown to pick up some material for a freelance medical writing assignment. As evidence of having achieved "flow" in my new life as a freelancer, the suit would work well for both the client meeting and the bachelor party.

The meeting went well. The article was for a "publishing" company, funded by an "educational grant" from the manufacturer of a relatively new cancer drug. I was to write a monograph that could be handed out to oncologists at a cancer meeting. The client, a 35-year-old balding guy who looked like a bouncer, handed me what he referred to as "a big pile of bullshit." It was mostly graphs from studies that compared different combinations of cancer drugs in patients with differing stages and grades of various kinds of tumors (e.g., breast, ovary, lung, prostate, colon) who may or may not have failed to respond favorably to various other regimens. The studies compared the outcomes of patients using drug combination XYZ versus drug combinations XYV and XYU, to show that patients did just the tiniest bit better whenever drug Z was used in place of drug V or drug U in otherwise identical combinations. For example, the five-year survival rate was 22% for drug combo XYZ vs. only 21% with XYV and 18% with XYU. These differences were "statistically significant"–and wasn't that cheerful news? The client responded to most of my questions by yawning and telling me the answer would probably become clear from the material.

The client said they would pay me $30 an hour and asked me how long it would take me. As far as I could see, all that was required was to put these graphs into some kind of intelligible order and slightly reword the captions, something that would take ten hours, fifteen hours tops. "Ballpark estimate, I'd say fifty hours," I said, trying to keep a straight face.

"Fifty hours? What, you kidding me?" the client blurted out and took a long slug of coffee. "I think you're living in a dream world. I think it's gonna take you at least a hundred hours. And just so you know, we bill the client fifty dollars an hour for your time, so don't rush it. Be thorough. Check and recheck your work." He winked at me.

Since the big pile of bullshit was far too large to fit into my briefcase, the client stuck it all in a big envelope and put that into a large plastic shopping bag. I was out on the street by 5 p.m. with two hours to kill. I phoned Rick, got his answering machine, and told him I'd be at the Arizona Bar and Grill, just a few blocks from his apartment. I went there, ordered a Corona, and began sipping it as I skimmed through the materials I'd been given.

At 7:10 p.m., Rick entered the Arizona Bar and Grill, clamped his hand down on my shoulder, and spun me around on the bar stool to face him. "Oh, great!" he exclaimed.

"What?"

"How many have you had?"

"I dunno. Four. Five. Maybe more. I dunno."

He grabbed my bar tab and began adding up entries: "My

God, it is absolutely amazing what you can accomplish in two hours!" Then he became distracted with the photo of the parrot. He grabbed it, stared at it, covered his eyes, and chuckled. "Okay, what's this?"

"Guy came in witha parrot, said he'd take my picture witha parrot on my shoulder for twenty bucks. So whassa big deal? Y'only live once, my man!"

I paid my bar tab and went with Rick to his apartment. As he got into his suit, I helped myself to a Budweiser out of his fridge. I figured it was rightfully mine, since it was left over from the six pack I brought to the last meeting at his house. Then Rick lit up some grass in a small pipe. "Say . . . " I muttered.

"Oh, this is just what you need! Trust me, after the day I've had, I need this. You don't want this, you don't need it. We'll be lucky if you even make it to the party at this rate."

After I turned down Rick's invitation to sleep on his sofa for a while, we cabbed it down to a bar in the East Village. I pulled out my wallet. Rick grabbed it out of my hand, took out a twenty, paid the cabdriver, put the change back into my wallet and slipped it back into the pocket of my jacket. We went inside.

The bar was filled with people I vaguely recognized: Judy. Peter's father. A friend of Peter's who worked at Nickelodeon. Some vaguely familiar-looking women. "Just do me a favor and stay away from the bar," Rick whispered in my ear and began hugging virtually everyone in the room as if they were old friends.

I sidled up to the bar, fished a fiver out of my wallet, and said, "Barkeep, a Corona, if you would."

The bartender looked me over, sighed, shook his head, and opened a Corona for me. I laid handed the fiver to him and told him to keep the change, seeing as how figuring out the change and tip would be much, much too complicated.

Peter's dad, a robust balding man in his early fifties, put his fingers to his lips and said, "Okay, everyone. Peter should be here any minute. And for Heaven's sake, be quiet!"

The 15 people in our midst crowded into a small back room, so close we were shoulder to shoulder and could smell each other's sweat. I was about to come up with some witty commentary on the situation, I'm sure, when Peter's dad poked his head around the corner, gestured the volume downward, and mouthed, "He's coming!" I looked at my watch. I squinted at my watch: It was nearly eight o'clock.

Suddenly everyone was yelling out "Surprise!" and the crowd surged forward like subway commuters when the doors open. It carried me into the main room like a raging river. The current carried me by a chair, which I grabbed, only to have it carried off with me, and fell to the floor in a crash. Rick shook his head and pulled me to my feet.

Peter beamed with surprise, and shook hands with everyone, although he had a very strange look on his face when he shook mine. "Surprise!" I called out, expecting him to react. He just smiled and nodded his head.

As people quizzed him about just exactly how surprised he was, I drifted to the back of the room and just absorbed the warm and fuzzy ambience of the gathering.

At about eight-thirty, it was time to roast Peter. This was a room full of comedy writers, so many of the roasts were excellent. I waited for a few moments of silence. Then, chuckling diabolically, I brought out a list of finely honed insults I had prepared earlier that day. Now everyone's attention was riveted on me.

The only problem was that the light was bad and my vision was now very, very blurry. My first roast made reference to the fact that Peter was a professional cartoonist. "When I . . . asked? . . . Peter . . . whether . . . there would be a . . . script? script art? no no no, strip act at his . . . bachelor party . . . he said . . . no. . . he didn't bring his . . . scratch? No no no. Oh, sketch pad!" I looked up with the victorious smile of a first-grader reading his first sentence aloud. Though I mangled the joke itself, the crowd enjoyed the delivery: Everyone was laughing uproariously.

I considered ad-libbing at this point. What material could I mine? Peter, his dad, Rick, Judy, and more than half the other attendees were Jewish. There ought to be something I could do with that. We were all friends, after all.

Peter patted me on the back, smiling, and gently pulled the list from my hands. "That was great, Rob!"

"I've got more!" I called out, and the crowd applauded.

"I'd love to hear them, but Rick requests your presence outside."

What was Rick plotting now? I wondered. Some new surprise for Peter? I struggled to my feet, patted Peter on the shoulders, and stumbled to the door.

"Thanks for coming!" he called out, which seemed to me a very strange thing to say, since I'd been there for nearly an hour.

Outside, Rick was standing in front of a cab. He opened the passenger door for me and then turned to the cabdriver. "Again, thank you. Thank you. The address is thirty-three fifty-four Twenty-Eighth Street in Astoria. He's got the money and he won't give you any problems, I swear." As he eased me into the seat, he said, "You've still got thirty bucks or so on you? Give it all to him when he drops you off–he'll have earned it." He gave me a hug, rubbed my hair for good luck, and said, "Have a safe trip home, buddy."

As the driver pulled out, he said in a affable British accent, "Quite the party, then, eh?"

"Yeah, bachelor party. For Peter. He's in my troupe."

"Troupe?"

"Yeah, comedy troupe. We been compared to Monty Python, right? You know Monty Python?"

He was fascinated, and wanted to know more. I told him about how we came together and our long and tortured history together. I just about had him up to date when I noticed the Hudson River to my left. "Say, what're we doin' on the Westside Highway, anyway?"

My head smashed against the plexiglass barrier as he screeched to a halt. "That's it! Get the fuck outta here!"

"What?"

"Trying to avoid midtown traffic is what I'm doing, and I've had it with you paranoid fucking drunks! Always thinking someone's trying to rip 'em off! I won't put up with it anymore! Get the fuck out of my cab!"

I got out and slammed the door, and the Brit sped uptown and out of sight. As I began the long trek toward Union Square, I found that my gait was better and my head was beginning to clear. That's when I passed the Old Town Tavern on Twelfth Street. In the 1920's, it had been a speakeasy and it still had a substantial wooden bar with a brass rail and heavy metal doors. God, I loved that bar. By now, my bladder was the size of a football, and I really, really didn't want to pee on the sidewalk. I went inside, and lo and behold, there was an empty bar stool. I set about finishing what I'd begun earlier that night, this time without the interference of friends.

That morning, I looked around frantically, in the bedroom, in the kitchen, in the living room, and the bathroom. I even walked down the stairs to the lobby. No briefcase. No big shopping bag full of bullshit.

I went upstairs to the ironing board in the bedroom, upon which sat Kari's old rotary phone whenever Kari wasn't ironing. I dialed Rick's number. When he picked up, I said, "Rick, it's Rob. Listen, I–"

"Yes, they're here. You almost left them in the Arizona Bar and Grill, but you probably don't remember that. You wanted to take them to the bachelor party, but I wouldn't let you take it. You probably don't remember that either. You don't remember a lot of things, I suspect."

"Listen, thank you so much. Are you going to be around this morning? Can I come pick them up?"

"I'll be here till two and then I'm heading out."

I took the subway into Manhattan, got off at 26th Street, and went to Rick's apartment, where he had my briefcase and shopping bag waiting. I thanked him, and as I was walking out the door with my stuff, he shook his head and said, "You are a fucking lunatic. I'm astonished you've made it this far, my friend."

When I got home, Kari was in her underwear, smoking a cigarette, drinking a cup of coffee, and ironing clothes all at the same time. "Hello," she chanted, not really looking up from her ironing. "Where were you?"

"Picking up some stuff I left at Rick's last night. Where were you?"

"Macy's. I want you to look at something."

She went and pulled something out of a Macy's bag. It was a black evening gown. "So, what do you think?"

"It's nice," I said. "What's it for?"

"The wedding, goober. Is your other suit pressed? Because I'm not letting you wear the one you wore last night."

"It's pressed."

"How was Peter's bachelor party?"

"Good, from what I can remember."

"What time did you leave?"

"About a quarter past eight."

"How come you were so late?"

"I stopped off at the Old Town Tavern for a couple of drinks on the way home. I had to pee really bad."

Kari let out a stage groan and said, "Robbie Robbie Robbie . . ." She ironed a few strokes and then said, "You had me worried. Rick called at eight-thirty to say he'd just put you into a cab."

"I'm sorry."

Peter and Nancy's wedding ceremony, held at a cozy function hall only a mile from our apartment, was warm, charming, and inclusive. Since Nancy was a Protestant, the Rabbi made it a point to carefully explain the significance of each ritual, such as holding up the hupa. I especially loved his explanation of stomping on the glass, which was a reminder of the fragility of marriage, of community, of life itself. Amen, brother.

Dinner was superb, I drank in moderation, and then there was dancing. As I held Kari tight during the slow dance, I looked around the room. Rick was dancing with some cute girl he'd met there, who had been sitting in his lap, and who seemed to love flirting with him even though she apparently knew he was gay. Rick smiled at me. Judy, Peter's father, and some of the strangers from the night before eventually made eye contact with me and smiled.

Then I looked up and saw Rose, dancing with Remy, smiling at me with this dreamy look in her eye. Angie too. None of these Chuckle-women had ever seen me dance with Kari, or any other woman, and they seemed happy for me.

For the time being, I had my friends. I had my clients. I had my health. I had my girlfriend. I did pretty much whatever I wanted. I didn't know how long it would all last, but for the moment, I was keeping it all together.

During a break from the dancing, Peter motioned me over with his typically benign smile. Since there was still plenty of ambient noise, and my hearing was frankly not the best, I had to put my ear right to his mouth. "I read the rest of your roasts aloud after you left, and everybody loved them! Will, my friend from Nickelodeon, especially liked them, and might have some work for you."

"That'd be great! Listen, I'm sorry about–"

"I want to say what a kick it was having you at my bachelor party, and in the condition that you were in!"

"I hope I wasn't too obnoxious!" I proclaimed loudly in his ear.

"Just obnoxious enough for a bachelor party! My other friends tend to be a little too . . . sober," he said, and added: "Of course, you can judge for yourself. I got the whole thing on video-tape. I'd be happy to show it to you sometime. You probably don't remember the videographer, do you?"

I turned toward him, and he was smiling harder than ever. Was he telling the truth? Had I really been so far gone that I didn't notice someone with a video camera? Or was there some evil edge to his personality that had eluded me all these years? To this day, I don't know whether he owns such a tape, nor have I ever asked to see it.

THE BLACK AND WHITE
WEDDING

In the back of my closet, I still have a box full of pictures of my wedding, all black and white, all in color. That is to say, it was a black and white wedding shot on color film stock. White dress. Black tuxedos. White shirts. Black dresses with white polka-dots. Arrangements of black roses and baby's breath on white table-cloths. A dark chocolate cake with white frosting. Black balloons and white balloons.

Darkness and light in an eternal struggle, with light prevailing over here and darkness winning over there and neither side fully gaining the upper hand. All tinted with the warm glow of candles, the murky red of Pinot Noir, the twinkle of blue and green eyes, the amber of beer, the blush of flushed cheeks.

Kari planned the details off the wedding, and her aunt helped her get everything at a discount. Someone's cousin took all the photos of the wedding, some posed and some candid, for only $600. There are more than 150 photos, all numbered and waiting to be placed in proper order in a wedding album, which never happened and never will.

Photo #11: Me in my black tux. Rick had helped me buy it in the garment district. He knew clothes. He had taken great delight in showing me which tuxes were generic rip-offs with designer labels sewn in. He steered me toward a simple, elegant, and inexpensive classic. In the picture, I am smiling but scared to death.

Photo #12: Me in the tux again, standing around nervously, with friends milling around nervously in the hotel suite behind me: Rick, my Best Man Dave, and my ex-coworker Kim, who is black and is dangerously close to fading from many of the photos. We had all spent the last two hours keeping me pleasantly distracted at a video arcade. While playing the "Gunfighter" game, I successfully gunned down a dozen bad guys who had kidnapped a young maiden. Unfortunately, I kept accidentally killing the maiden as well. Oops.

Photo #15: Rick adjusting my tie, while his companion Jack looks on. Seconds later, he broke it, with just minutes to spare before we had to rush over to the wedding. He disappeared for half a minute, returned with a needle and thread, and had the tie sewn back together within two minutes. He had nerves of steel that night because he was high on smack.

Photo #19: The Mount Washington tour boat in Center Harbor, New Hampshire, where the wedding was held. It is a well-known and mammoth presence on Lake Winnipesaukee. It is early May. It is dusk, it is drizzling, and the water is black, but a warm glow radiates from the windows of the Mount.

Photo #22: The Captain, a portly, jovial gent in his late sixties. He was also the Justice of the Peace and the leader of the wedding band.

Photo 27: Kari's Maid of Honor, Alena, smiling and holding up a sheet of Dramamines.

Photo #28: Kari, looking angelic in her lacy white wedding gown, lighting a cigarette.

Photo #42: Me standing with my brother and father, both in black tuxes too. All three of our ties are crooked, but we're all too oblivious by nature to notice. My brother Richard is smiling, even though he just found out his wife had cancer, but his cheeks look sunken.

Photo #45: My Best Man Dave, looking like the investment banker that he is, taking a nip from a flask of Johnny Walker to calm his nerves. He offered me a nip, too, but I didn't take it, as

I'd promised Kari I wouldn't drink before the wedding.

Photo #49: My sister, wearing a black dress with white polka dots, crying.

Photos #52-54: Kari and I, standing in front of the Captain, reciting our wedding vows. Kari lifted some good stuff from Shelley and Corinthians I.

Photo #55: Man and wife kiss.

Photo #61: Kari and I taking our places at the center of the wedding party table. Everyone is smiling and applauding. It is an intimate group of about 80 people.

Photo #63: Rick with his arms wrapped around Kari, both grinning. Misty-eyed and in a tux, Rick looks like a big-name crooner from the 1940s.

Photo #67: Mom and Kari, hugging each other.

Photo #75: My timid former boss Erika looking uncomfortable. Sitting right next to her, Spanky is groping and tongue-kissing his gorgeous new coke-slut girlfriend, whom I had to invite at the last minute.

Photos #82-88: Everyone in the wedding party dancing with virtually everybody else in the wedding party.

Photo #90: Jim dancing with Angie, dressed in a black party dress and exotically patterned black hose. Ouch!

Photo #91: Spanky dancing with Angie.

Photo #92: Dirk dancing with Angie.

Photo #93. Me dancing with Rose.

Photo #94: Me dancing with Judy.

Photo #95: Me and Angie. At first glance, we appear to be dancing with each other, but it's an illusion: We're looking off in opposite directions, apparently talking to other people.

Photo #97: Remy and Rose pressed together, dancing. He's a foot taller than she is. He's looking down over his wire-rim glasses at her, and she's looking straight up at him. It's a slow dance, but they're smoldering at each other and look ready to tango.

Photo #99: My Best Man dancing with my sister. In the foreground, Dirk is break-dancing on the floor or feigning sudden death. It's hard to tell which.

Photo #105. Rick and my mother smiling warmly at each other. He later described her as beautiful and elegant. Mom found him the most handsome and engaging of all the Chuckleheads and said he had a "warm glow" about him. I never had the heart to tell her where the warm glow came from.

Photo #103: All the Chuckleheads break-dancing. The Captain looks baffled. I've had a few drinks now and my hair has fallen sloppily into Moe Howard bangs. My brother Richard, a clinical psychologist, is standing at the edge of the dance floor, watching with detached interest. He later said, "Your friends really remind me of some of my bipolar patients. Not that that's a bad thing."

Photo#105-108: Kari and I cutting the cake and feeding pieces to each other. Conspicuously absent is anybody mashing cake into anybody else's face.

Photos#110-114: Rick dancing with Angie, Rose, Judy, my sister, and my mother, respectively.

Photo#119: Rick patting his companion Jack on the back. They look like old football buddies.

Photo #120: Angie telling an animated story to Spanky and Rose, feigning a look of total shock. It could have been an incident from this weekend or something that happened at an audition in New York. Who knows?

Photo #121: Me throwing Kari's garter to a mob of bachelors. Rick and Dirk, both with cigarettes hanging out of their mouths, seem poised not to catch it.

Photo #122: Spanky jumps up and snags the garter, like a basketball player tipping the ball into the hoop.

Photo #123: The tossing of the bouquet. A lot of pretty young single women–including Angie, Rose, Judy, the Maid of

Honor, and Spanky's girlfriend–are there to catch it.

Photo #124: Kari's brassy 68-year-old divorced step-grandmother deftly catching the bouquet.

Photo #125: Spanky putting Kari's white garter on her step-grandmother's leg, as the crowd cheers for him to move it higher and higher on her leg. She's enjoying it, but even after years of acting classes, Spanky isn't smiling convincingly. Standing in the background, my former boss Erika appears to be gloating.

Photo #152: Kari and I sitting on the dark-carpeted stairs, intertwined and beaming. Black and white jut, swirl, and splatter all over each other. We look like a very artistic but hastily rendered ink drawing.

Photo #153: The last remaining Chuckleheads–Dirk, Jim, Angie, Rose, Spanky, Rick, Peter, Judy, Paul, and myself–posing together on the stairs. It was the last time we were all in the same photograph.

ROB DINSMOOR

REQUIEM FOR
SEA CAPTAIN FRANK

Monday

Naked, Kari was simultaneously trying to iron her work clothes, smoke a cigarette, and drink a cup of coffee. I was transfixed, as usual: I was sure she'd burn herself one way or another, but how?. "So, how's the script coming?" she asked.

She was referring to the script I was assembling from individual scenes for Chucklehead's upcoming show, "Stocks and Prawns" at the most esteemed off-off-Broadway theatre in New York, LeMama. The show was Friday and we were still patching the script together.

I sighed, trying to get it all into focus. The half a cup of coffee I'd had so far was just beginning to cut through my fog. Kari's black cat Ouzo, who had recently become my cat, climbed onto my bare chest and purred seductively in my ear. Our new tortoise-shell kitten, Mud Bug, was apparently hiding somewhere. In fact, she was incredibly adept at finding secret hiding places and disappearing for hours inside our tiny two-bedroom apartment.

"It's totally out of control," I finally said. "This is what happens when you write a script by committee."

I described the collection of scenes and characters and ideas that made up the so-called "plot." It started with a troupe of performance artists who couldn't decide which direction to take their upcoming show. (Sound familiar?) One of the performance artists quits to join the corporate world in the form of an oil conglomerate known as Noble Oil. Noble Oil's CEO is not so much a person as a giant, flickering face on a screen and a thundering disembodied voice. Noble Oil's mascot is Sea Captain Frank, played by Spanky in a long brown beard and captain's outfit, who is the "sure and steady" captain of one of Noble Oil's tankers. That is, when he doesn't have the shakes.

Sea Captain Frank is in fact a terrible alcoholic. We wrote this right after the Exxon Valdez disaster. I didn't think we should just make Sea Captain Frank a carbon copy of Hazelwood, so I penned scenes in which Sea Captain Frank buggers his men when they're at the helm. It is during a wild party and one of these "trysts" that the tanker hits an iceberg and creates the worst oil spill in history. (Crashing noise. Blackout. "Uh oh.")

From there, the plot begins to turn weird: It involves giant bioengineered oil-eating shrimp; the disappearance and reappearance of Sea Captain Frank; assassination attempts on Sea Captain Frank by clumsy, anally retentive Noble Oil executives, disguised as Arab terrorists, who view Sea Captain Frank as a public relations nightmare; Alan Hale Junior's Seafood Sauce; a wildly fluctuating stock market based on the ever-changing fate of Noble Oil; a couple of smarmy news anchors; and even an audience participation interval in which audience members get to trade their shares of Noble Oil and Alan Hale Junior's Seafood Sauce. All of the performers were to play multiple roles.

Dirk faxed over scene changes after every rehearsal, and incorporating them all in the master script, which was my responsibility, became a full-time job. My Leading Edge Model D, like every other electronic device in my life, was notoriously unreliable. Sometimes it saved all the changes to the script and sometimes it didn't. I constantly backed up each draft on a floppy disk, but sometimes I wasn't sure which draft was the latest one.

"Poor sweetie," was all Kari could say. She threw on her outfit, glanced at the full-length mirror leaning against the wall next to the ironing board, and took a contemplative drag from her cigarette.

"What time is your flight?"

"Five-thirty. I'm going to ditch work early and cab it to LaGuardia."

After Kari left for work, I got down to the business of updating the script. At the rehearsal the night before, while the performers were rehearsing certain scenes, Dirk scribbled changes on his copy of the script and handed it to me. It was my job to amend the script every few days, re-date it on the front page, print it out, have it photocopied, and bring it to rehearsal.

An hour later, after I finished amending the script, I saved it onto a floppy disk. Next, from my briefcase, I fished out an ad for a breathalyzer Dirk had torn out of a police gazette and given me the night before. I was supposed to make one. Props were usually Spanky's bailiwick but he was already overcommitted, so I volunteered to do it. After studying the picture carefully, I went on a shopping spree in Astoria and Long Island City.

Outside, it was sunny and the sky was a rich blue color, but it was also cold and blustery. From my apartment in Astoria, I walked several blocks north to Steinway Street, the local shopping Mecca. There, in a variety store, I bought a toy ray gun and a can of black spray paint. Two doors down, at a cigar store, I bought a big box of Dutch Masters cigars. From there, I walked toward the Queensborough Bridge in Long Island City.

Taking the ten-minute walk from Astoria to Long Island City was like tumbling head-first down the socioeconomic ladder. Nice apartment buildings and corner stores quickly gave way to cheap housing developments, warehouses, chop shops, and the occasional strip club and methadone clinic. After a few minutes, I located a medical-surgical supply house and emerged with a length of surgical tubing. I kept all my receipts.

Back at my apartment, I laid down newspapers on the kitchen floor and spray-painted the empty cigar box black. When it dried, I cut a round hole in the top and stuck in eight inches of

surgical tubing. I cut off part of the grip of the ray gun. I cut a section out of the back of the cigar box and duct –taped the ray gun
halfway inside it–with the plastic tip of the ray gun sticking out the
top of the box. Since it didn't look quite right, I took a label from a
box of floppy disks and stuck it on the front. Now it looked official.

As the paint was drying, I got a call from Dirk. "Did you
make the script changes?" he asked.

"Yup."

"Are the batteries for your video camera charged?"

"I don't know. Why?"

"We still need the video footage of Sea Captain Frank at
sea, and Paul can't do it before Friday. We need you to meet Spanky
and me down at the entrance to the Staten Island Ferry with all
your equipment in an hour and a half. Think you can do it?"

A feeling of panic swept over me. Staten Island was about
as far from Astoria as you could get, and I would have to leave
within half an hour. And what the hell were we doing videotaping
segments a mere four days before we were slated the premiere at
the top off-off-Broadway theatre in the city? Furthermore, my second-hand video camera and deck had a history of battery failure,
microphone failure, color inconsistencies, you name it. I had
bought it to give me some leverage over making videos for the
show, and it had ended up being my albatross.

"Sure. Except you know my video camera is notoriously
unreliable. I just want you to realize that," I said.

"Well, let me just make a suggestion. Just show up with all
your equipment, and if any of it fails, I'll just throw it and you into
New York harbor."

I spent the next half hour collecting and checking my
video equipment. The camera's battery still worked, for now.
Videotape in video deck? Check. Spare tape? Check. Microphone?
Check. Headphones? Check. Everything seemed in order.

Minutes later, I was lugging two twenty-five-pound bags

up the stairs to the Broadway subway platform in Astoria. In one bag, I carried the video deck, cables, microphone, and two spare camera batteries, and in the other, I had the video camera, the amended script, and my newly minted breathalyzer.

Roughly an hour later, I got off at Wall Street and walked over to the Staten Island Ferry. I was about five minutes late. Dirk and Spanky were already there with their own duffle bags of crap.

Once we boarded, we went up on the upper deck and started preparing for our guerilla video shoot. As the ferry made its way toward Staten Island, we were treated to a great view of the island of Manhattan, which had never looked so crisp, clean, and beautiful. It was mid-afternoon, the sky was still deep blue, the sun was just starting to think about setting, and the angle of reddening sunlight accentuated the edges of all the skyscrapers, especially the Twin Towers. Yet, we really couldn't take the time to look at that now. In fact, we had to make sure that none of the Manhattan sky-line made it into the frame, because Sea Captain Frank was supposed to be far out at sea.

The briny ocean breeze stung my hands and tickled my nostrils as I took my video equipment out of the two bags and began piecing it together. I was relieved when I actually turned the camera on and got an image—and there was no blinking "low battery" sign in the viewfinder. Next, I plugged headphones into the earphone jack and then plugged the microphone into the microphone jack.

No sound was coming through the microphone.

I clicked it off and on several times, but still not a sound. I looked at it, and then opened up a small compartment, inside which was a double-A Duracell battery. A dead double-A Duracell battery, to be precise. Who the hell would have known there were batteries inside a microphone, for God's sake?

Paul would have, I thought. I began rifling through both bags, but couldn't find any batteries.

"What are you looking for?" Dirk asked.

"A piece of gum," I lied.

I continued rifling till I looked up and saw a stick of Spearmint hovering in front of my face. "Here you go, man," Dirk said.

Even though gum was the last thing I wanted right then, I took it, unwrapped it, and put it in my mouth. By this time, Spanky was already wearing his Captain's jacket, Captain's hat, and big, bushy brown beard, and people were passing by and staring at him. "Hey, I forget. Do I have any lines in this thing?"

"No, man. It's all silent. Paul's going to edit all the shots into a PR montage for Noble Oil and lay a voice-over on top of it," Dirk explained.

When all this sank in, I heaved a sigh of relief, put the microphone and headphones away, and said, "All set on this end."

Simultaneously, I videotaped short takes and Dirk took still photos of Sea Captain Frank: Sea Captain Frank staring out over the ocean, his eyes squinting as if he were mentally charting the safest route to take. Sea Captain Frank, his hair ruffling in the ocean breeze, saluting the camera. Sea Captain Frank leaning over a railing, squinting into a pair of binoculars. At one point, a mother and two kids passed into the frame and Sea Captain Frank winked at them and saluted. In all the shots, Sea Captain Frank had a solid and impenetrable affect, and we shot him from a low angle to make him look tall and imposing.

About 45 minutes into shooting, the "low battery" light started flashing. We were shooting Sea Captain Frank smoking a pipe and squinting at an enormous map. By this time, about a dozen tourists were hanging out and gaping at us. Did they think this was street theater? Did they think this was for their benefit? Why didn't they go look at skyscrapers or something?

Then the viewfinder went black. "Cut!" Dirk shouted. I pretended to press the camera's trigger to stop taping. "Let's call it a wrap. It's starting to get dark anyway."

I breathed a sigh of relief. I had just squeaked through that one.

"Shit, it's about time. My nose has been running and I'm starting to get snot in my beard," Spanky announced, and some of the spectators laughed.

"Can I see what we've shot?" Dirk asked.

"No, I don't want to wear down the battery."

"Can my children have their picture taken with you?" one lady asked. And, of course, Spanky obliged. While Spanky posed with the kids, Dirk took a quick photo of them too, and I wondered if that picture would make it into the show.

It was twilight when we made it back to dry land again. As Dirk had arranged, we met Paul at the Acme Bar and Grill around 6 p.m. There, amidst the din of conversation and the clatter of pans in the kitchen reverberating off the Acme's brick walls, we dined on catfish, grits, black-eyed peas, and Rolling Rocks. We handed the film and videotape over to Paul, who then drove back to New Jersey and would spend a good part of the night editing the scenes together and laying down the voice over.

Next, after stopping off at Gingko's to make 10 copies of the updated script, Dirk and I headed over to LeMama, which was only a few blocks away. "Did you get a chance to make the breathalyzer?" Dirk asked, and I whipped it out of my bag and demonstrated its use to the cast.

While I blew into the surgical tubing, I pulled the trigger on the ray gun, which was concealed behind the painted cigar box. The tip of the ray gun lit up and, as I squeezed the trigger harder, glowed red, and the contraption made an electronic noise that crescendoed. As far as I know, this is not something that breathalyzers actually do, but I felt they really *ought* to.

Up close, it was just a black-spray-painted cigar box with tubing and a toy ray gun stuck to the back of it. But, from a distance, it was a diverting gizmo. The cast loved it, and everyone took turns playing with it.

It belonged in the scene where, before Sea Captain Frank rams into an iceberg, he's having a wild party on the ship. Everyone, including an airline pilot who is about to go on duty (Rick) is drinking way too much. They're passing around the breathalyzer as sort of a party game.

It's a scene where we writers fill in as extras. Jim holds the breathalyzer as Rick blows into it, and then reads it. "Point one. He's legally drunk! Do me next!"

Rick holds the breathalyzer while Jim blows into it. "One point 'O. He's legally dead!"

Jim laughs and passes out cold.

"Uh oh!" I say. "We'd better get the ship's doctor!"

"That was the ship's doctor!" Peter says.

Badump-ski. "Very Mad Magazine," Dirk said of the scene. "But that's okay. It works."

After rehearsing this scene and passing out copies of the new script, I hopped on an N Train at Astor Place and headed back to Astoria. When I got home, around 9:30 p.m., there were marked up pages of the script in my fax tray (where did they come from and when?) and a message blinking on my answering machine. I pressed the button to play it.

"Hi, it's me," said the voice of Kari. "I've found a house I really like, and I think you'll love it too. Can you take the shuttle up here tomorrow? Give me a call."

For months, there had been talk of Chucklehead disbanding. Pat and Russell had both left the troupe and, despite mostly good reviews, good things just weren't happening for us as a group. Yet, Dirk and Jim were now firmly ensconced in jobs writing and producing at Nickelodeon. Meanwhile, I had taken the plunge into freelance writing, which I could do from anywhere. So, there was very little keeping me in New York. And Kari hated the city. Hated it.

She had asked whether, the next time she visited her sister in a small town in Massachusetts, she could look for a house she liked. I had said, sure, go for it. And so now she had.

I called her back at her sister's. She asked me to fly up the next morning on the 10:00 shuttle so she could show me the house. "It's a cute little turn-of-the-century Victorian with a front porch and a back staircase, and even a spare bedroom that can be your office—and all these weird angles!" she raved. "You'll love it! Bring your checkbook!"

Exhausted, I agreed to all of the above and then fished a beer out of the fridge.

The phone rang and I answered it. "Kari?"

"It's Paul. I'm looking over the footage you shot. On that one shot you took on the bow of the ferry, did you by any chance have the aperture set on 'manual?'"

I felt a gnawing sensation in my stomach. "I don't remember."

"I think you must have. It produced this really weird sort of hazy-fog effect that's really cool. In fact, all the footage looks great. Good job! I just wanted to tell you that. I have a few more hours of editing to do."

"Thanks. Good luck."

I drank beers as I watched my video of "The Terminator" until I could no longer follow the plot. Then I went to bed.

Tuesday

I awoke around 8:30 a.m., slightly disoriented—partly because Kari wasn't beside me, but also because I'd spent the entire night having dreams that I'd bought the house I grew up in—a turn-of-the-century Victorian very similar to what Kari had described. The dream was a veritable tour of the house and all its quirks—the coal bin, the giant register that led down to hell, the picture window, the thorny trellis of roses, the scary basement furnace with its eight arms that rose up to the ceiling.

As I took my shower, I thought I heard a gnawing sound. At first I thought it was the cats gnawing on a piece of dry cat food they had dragged in from their bowls. But each time I pulled back the shower curtain, there was no cat or anything else in the room with me.

Remembering what I had to do, I quickly ate a bowl of cereal, packed an overnight bag, and made changes to the script from the pages that lay in my fax tray. Then I called a cab, took a 15-minute ride to LaGuardia, and hopped aboard the shuttle to Boston. The take-off afforded a beautiful view of the Manhattan skyline, and the Empire State Building, visible out my kitchen window just half an hour earlier, seemed close enough to touch from the plane. Was I really ready to leave it all?

Kari met me at the gate at Logan, escorted me to a cab, which we took to North Station to catch the 11:30 train to Hamilton. On the way, I told her how the show was going and we generally caught up on things.

We walked from the train station down a sleepy main street lined with a post office, a dentist's office, a hardware store, and a tiny restaurant called The Weathervane Tavern. Shades of Mayberry!

We took a right, and then a left onto Rust Street. Young, well-dressed Caucasian moms pushed strollers down the street without a care in the world. People walked dogs, well-fed cats stalked back and forth across the street, and squirrels scrambled around on front lawns. As we were walking down it, Kari pointed to one of the houses and said, "That's it."

It really was a delightful Victorian house. It had a front porch, a side porch, a separate concrete garage, and small front and back lawns. More and more, it reminded me of the house where I grew up. We met the real estate lady, who showed us the inside.

By three o'clock, I was writing a check for $700, which was "earnest money" to say that we were interested in buying the house. I wrote down an offer of $150,000, which seemed to me a staggering amount of money. The real estate lady promised to fax me a list of potential mortgage lenders.

I took the 4:32 train into Boston, took a cab to Logan, and caught the 6 p.m. shuttle to LaGuardia, still dazed that I seemed to be buying a house. As I flew in toward LaGuardia, looking down at Manhattan was like looking up in the sky on a clear night: You could see thousands of tiny points of light and imagine millions of possibilities. Was I ready to leave?

At LaGuardia, I caught a cab and gave him my address in Astoria. By the time we were on the Long Island Expressway, I had changed my mind and asked him to take me to LeMama in the East Village. I was completely wired up and not ready to go back to an empty apartment.

When I got to LeMama around 8 p.m., the cast cheered my arrival. Something was up. "Where have you been? Did you get my message? We didn't know if you'd make it or not," Dirk said.

"I didn't get any message. I haven't been to my apartment since this morning. I was up buying a house in Massachusetts."

Dirk blinked a couple of times, assimilating this information, but he stayed focused on the events at hand. "Listen, we need you to familiarize yourself with Rick's part and fill in for him, at least for tonight's rehearsal."

"What's going on?"

"Rick's in jail," Dirk explained.

"My God! What—"

"We don't know all the details. Jack called us from work, and he's on his way now to bail him out now. He's definitely not making it tonight, and we just don't know whether he's going to be able to do the show at this point," Dirk said, and shoved a copy of the script in my hand. "We highlighted all Rick's lines and we'll walk you through it tonight. I hope you're a quick study."

I was the furthest thing from a quick study. I immediately

started to hyperventilate.

I dutifully stood in each of Rick's scenes and delivered the lines as best I could, but the whole thing reminded me of my recurring nightmare in which, unbeknownst to me until the last minute, my high school drama club is doing an alumni benefit and I have a small role—and I have to memorize my lines between scenes. As I walked through Rick's parts, people would gently turn me and walk me in this or that direction while Dirk barked directions as patiently as he could. I tried to write down the stage directions on the script, like "Enter SR, X to Angie, XL SL door," some of which were crossed out with arrows pointing to other stage directions. I knew the whole thing would be totally incomprehensible to me by Wednesday.

Whenever I started to imagine that I could pull it off, I remembered that there would be involved costume changes between each of these scenes.

I took the N train back to Astoria, and got home around 11 p.m. There were two messages on my answering machine—one from Dirk, asking me to come to the meeting, and the other one was from Kari. Kari said the owners of the house had come back with a counter-offer of $160,000 and what should we do? She said she'd be back early tomorrow morning and we could discuss it then. In my fax tray were changes to the script and a list of mortgage lenders and their phone numbers.

When I went into the bathroom, I heard that gnawing sound again. This time, I could tell it was coming from the wall. Was it a rat? That's when I saw the bubbles in the wallpaper. The sound I was hearing was the wallpaper slowly peeling away from the wall. I looked up at the ceiling to see a damp brown spot. There was a leak somewhere.

I phoned Jose, the super, who was gone as usual. I left a message on the machine telling him to hurry on over. There was an emergency.

Drinking one beer after another, I read and re-read Rick's lines until my vision blurred, and I went to bed.

Wednesday

I awoke to the sound of Kari ironing clothes. She explained that she had taken a very early shuttle and was going to work. I told her everything that had happened, and she was appalled, most of all by what had happened to Rick. I told her I'd keep her posted. "What should we do in the way of a counter-offer?" she asked.

"Can I think about it?"

"Okay, but don't wait too long. We don't want to blow this."

After she left for work, I immediately went to work adding the latest corrections to the script, some of which were Rick's lines. Oh well. Then I spent an hour trying to memorize Rick's lines. The last time I actually had to memorize lines was in a high school play, and I used the same trick now as I did then. I covered up the lines with a piece of cardboard and kept testing myself on each line until I got it right, word for word, and then moved on to the next one. I got through the script in two hours, and I was fried.

Then I began calling the mortgage companies off the list and finding out their percentage rates on a 30-year mortgage. Thirty years ! Thirty years seemed like a long time, since I'd only been on the planet for 32. When I had spoken with or at least left messages with all the institutions on the list, I returned to memorizing Rick's lines.

This time I tried to see if I could get through the entire script. So, I started with the first one and decided to see how far I could get. I played the masochistic game of starting over from the beginning each time I screwed up. Within another hour, I had flubbed dozens of times, and had only made it a quarter of the way through the script on my best shot.

At 6:30, I made my way to the subway. Kari was just coming down the stairs as I was coming up. "Off to rehearsal?" she asked.

"Where else?"

"Will I see you tonight?"

"When you going to bed?"

"Probably around ten."

"Probably not, then."

"Well, did you think about the counter-offer?"

"Let's offer her one fifty-five."

"Okay. I'll call the real estate lady tonight."

"Listen—I should probably tell you—there's a leak in the apartment above ours and all the wallpaper is coming off in the bathroom. I'm expecting Jose to stop by and look at it."

"What?"

"See you tomorrow morning," I said, kissing her. And off we went on our separate ways.

I felt tense and nauseated as soon as I set foot in LeMama. Dirk looked extremely tense and irritable. Since this was only the second to last rehearsal before the show went up, Dirk took the script away from me and had Peter cue me. It was a nightmare. I needed to be prompted for virtually every other line, making me feel like Peter's ventriloquist dummy, Dirk was glaring and snapping stage directions at me, and I resented not having the script, all of which totally screwed up my concentration.

Throughout the rehearsal, Paul was engaged in getting the technical side of the show mounted. He had a slide projector apparently designed by NASA, which could rapidly show three slides at a time in a preprogrammed sequence. It was so fast moving between slides that it could produce a sort of animation effect. He had three slides of a crosshair projecting simultaneously and spent a good 20 minutes getting the crosshairs to align perfectly in a single image. Meanwhile, Jim was practicing the songs, transitions, and codas on his Casio.

It was pure chaos. It was the way rehearsals always went, but I was simply not used to it and it was throwing me off.

Judy arrived with hundreds of copies of the program she'd designed and printed out. She handed them out to us for our approval. "Oh, wow! These look really great!" Angie said. Everyone muttered their assents.

Paul took a brief break from his high-tech project and picked up the program. He smiled at the cover, but his gaze darkened as soon as he opened it up. Beneath the expressionless mask that composed his face, I could see mandibular muscles flexing against each other so hard it looked like his right eyeball would pop out, his temples would implode, and his jaw fly out of its socket. I had never seen him so angry. "Dirk, we need to talk. Now," he said.

"Can it wait? I'm right in the middle of this scene," Dirk said.

"No."

The tone made Dirk take notice. "All right, man."

They went downstairs to the dressing room. I could hear both of them shouting, but I couldn't make out the words. "What are they saying? Can you hear?" I asked Angie.

"No. Who knows? Who cares?" she said, and when I looked puzzled, she said, "Things have been tense between them all week."

"What's it over?"

"They're guys. It must be some kind of pissing contest."

Paul stormed back into the room, followed by Dirk, who was shouting, "Paul! Wait up, man!"

"Good luck putting the show up without slide projectors!" Paul shouted. He yanked the plug on the projector and started cramming it into his bag, before reason took over and he gently and lovingly packed the components away.

"Paul, what's going on, man?" Spanky, dressed as Sea Captain Frank, asked.

"There's no show. That's what's going on!"

"Paul, man. Calm down and tell me what's happening."

"I don't want to talk about it." Paul carried away the bag with his slide projector.

Everyone turned to Dirk. "What's going on?" Spanky asked.

"I don't want to talk about it," Dirk said, pouting.

"Paul said there wasn't going to be a show."

"Oh, there'll be a show all right. Let's get back to rehearsing the scene."

We continued the scene we were rehearsing, but we were all very distracted, most of all Dirk. In fact, I was forgetting my lines left and right and just repeating everything Peter told me like a robot, but Dirk didn't seem to care.

At the end of the rehearsal, Dirk took Judy aside and whispered to her. "What? What?" she snapped. "That's ridiculous! No way! I'm not doing it!" Then she stormed out, too.

On our way to the subway, I asked her what the conversation was all about, but I already knew what she would say: "I don't want to talk about it."

When I got home, Kari was already asleep. I turned on the TV, cracked a beer, and mindlessly read Rick's lines over and over again as if they would somehow sink in by themselves. Two hours later, when I awoke with a crick in my neck, I decided it was time to go to bed.

Thursday

I awoke to pounding on the door. I looked up at the digital clock on the ironing board. It was already 9:30 a.m. Kari must have decided to let me sleep. I slipped into my bathrobe and answered the door. It was Jose, a young Hispanic male in his early thirties, and two of his henchmen. "Robert, let me see what you are talking about."

I showed him the wallpaper, which was now starting to billow out from the wall. The brown spot on the ceiling had gotten wider and browner and was now dripping a puddle on the floor. Jose murmured something to one of his henchmen, and then the other, in Spanish. "This is very serious," he said to me gravely, as if I were the one who was remiss in my duties. "I'm going to turn the water main off and then go in."

Go in? What did that mean? Soon, one of the henchmen returned with a couple of picks and the two of them began smashing the plaster, sending chunks of it into the bathtub, sink, and toilet. As I went back to work, I saw both cats huddled under my desk. I wanted to be there with them.

As the banging continued, I tried again to make myself memorize Rick's lines, but to no avail. Every time I tried to dredge up a line from the back of my mind, a loud percussion would jar it irretrievably from my head. I went into the kitchen and, as I poured myself the first cup of coffee of the morning, the coffee mug was rattling against the pot. I actually considered pouring myself a tall glass of vodka to calm my nerves, but the idea scared me so much, I put it out of my mind.

When the percussions stopped, I realized my ears were ringing. Jose came into the kitchen, panting and sweating. "Robert," he wheezed. "We've located the problem. There's a plumbing leak in the apartment above. We're going upstairs to fix it, and we'll be back later to fix the hole."

I checked out the hole. They had ripped out a swatch of tile and wall that was about three feet in diameter, roughly a foot off the floor. Kari would flip out. I settled back into memorizing, memorizing, memorizing. There was a pit in my stomach.

I still had a pit in my stomach when I arrived at LeMama early that evening. I dreaded the tension between Dirk and Paul and I absolutely dreaded stumbling through Rick's lines and getting yelled at.

Yet, when I stepped into the lobby, I heard barking, and realized Rick was there. In fact, when I came into the theatre, everything seemed miraculously back to normal. The cast was milling around haphazardly, Paul was calmly setting up his slide projector, and Judy was taking programs out of a cardboard box. Rick was on stage, taking script changes from Dirk.

"Rick!" I called out, practically on the verge of tears. "Am I ever glad to see you!"

"I'll bet!" he said. "They told me you were going to try to fill in for me. Boy, would I love to be in that audience!"

"Are these new programs?" I asked Judy.

"Yeah."

"Why did you have to make new ones?"

Judy sighed and handed me two copies of the program. They looked pretty much identical. Except . . . in the old version, Dirk was listed as the director of the show, and in the newer version he wasn't. I looked up from the program to Judy, who just smiled, shrugged at me, and said, "Your tax dollars at work."

I figured it out. Paul had put his all into the show and was rightfully listed as the "Techno Tsar." But, after all the additional work he'd put in, sometimes pulling all-nighters to edit the footage into the proper sequence, he just couldn't abide Dirk giving himself the "Director" billing and it had become a big bone of contention. Somehow, however, possibly through Judy's arbitration, the whole thing had gotten smoothed out and we were good to go again.

From the pay phone in the lobby, I called Kari to tell her that Rick was okay, but the first thing out of her mouth was, "Did you know our bathroom's a goddamn cave?"

"Yeah, I forgot to tell you. Jose said he's be back to fix it."

"When?"

"I don't know. I just called to tell you Rick's okay."

"I'll bet you're relieved. Give him a hug for me," she said, and then her voice took on a more solemn tone. "Say, when was the last time you saw Mud Bug?"

"This morning, when Jose and the boys came in. Why?"

"I haven't seen her since I got home."

I rattled off a number of Mud Bug's favorite hiding places, such as under the sink, the cupboard, the back of the closet, and inside the arm of the fold-out couch, but she said she's looked at all of them. "I'm afraid she's gotten into the walls," Kari finally said.

Even though the prospect of her disappearing into the ninth dimension scared the hell out of me, I tried to sound reassuring. "Don't worry. If she can get herself into the walls, she can get herself out."

After we rehearsed the one scene I was in, I went down to the dressing room and began doing one of my crossword puzzles. Rick came down, took off his jacket, and looked quizzically at my puzzle. He still seemed shaken up. "It's from the Crossword of the Month Club. They send you ten crossword puzzles each month—the kind you'd see in the Sunday New York Times magazine."

"I love the Sunday New York Times crosswords," he said, pleadingly.

I handed him one. "Here, take it."

"Are you sure?"

"I've got ten of them!"

Rick started work on his. "I really need this to help calm me down."

"Rough week, huh?"

"Let me just say of anyone offers you a night in jail cell in this city, don't do it. It's disgusting. Think of being handcuffed to a urinal in the men's room at Penn Station overnight, and you'll start to have an idea of it. And you would not believe the vile stuff that's written on jail cell walls. When I got out, I was taking showers, like, every half an hour. But that wasn't even the worst part," Rick began.

"The weird thing was, I was only about a block from my

house, so I felt safe. There's a park where all the dealers hang out–one of my Iranian friends at the corner deli told me about it. So, I went to buy a bag of smack, and the guy turned out to be a narc. Suddenly, in fact, I'm surrounded by three narcs, all rushing in on me like they were a SWAT team and I'd just opened fire on a playground or something.

"Well, they handcuff me, shove me into the back of a police car, you know, with the metal grating right in front of my face. And they confiscate my backpack, with all my shit in it. And, so, these two real serious slimeball cops are sitting in the front seat, looking through my stuff. And one of 'em goes, 'Chucklehead, what's that?' So, I explain to him that it was this comedy troupe, that we're doing a show at LeMama, and in fact I'm supposed to be at a rehearsal in two hours. Then I just break down, sobbing like a baby.

"Then one of the slimeballs gets hold of my head shot, holds the photo up to the steel grate, then shows it to the other scumbag and says, 'Look how he's smiling in this photo. What's wrong, laughing boy? I don't see you smiling now!' Things just don't get much worse than that.

"The good news is that I talked to a court-appointed attorney, who was really busy but a stand-up lady. She said she's pretty sure she can get the case thrown out. One, because it was really sort of entrapment, and two, because of the way I was treated. Probably the worst that will happen is I'll be in a rehab program and have to go to a methadone clinic."

I patted him on the shoulder and said, "It's great to have you back–and not just because I couldn't memorize your lines."

When I got back to the apartment, I opened a beer. On the fridge was a note: "Still no sign of Mud Bug. Can you look for her before you go to bed?"

I went into the living room and turned on the TV to low volume–but I couldn't watch it because of an obsessive thought in my head. I got a flashlight out of the hall closet and went into the bathroom. I turned it on and peered into the hole, where I could just make out a pipe a few inches below. Below that, there was nothing–possibly just thin air. And then I heard a faint mewing. "Mud Bug! Here, Mud Bug!" I called out, somewhat quietly to avoid waking Kari. And again, I heard a faint cry in response. Sometimes I thought I could see a couple of tiny shiny orbs many feet away in the dark, but convinced myself it was my imagination. I kept this up for about twenty minutes before deciding to go to bed.

As I climbed into bed, Kari kissed me and asked, "Did you look for Buggie?"

"Yeah."

"Did you find her?"

"No. Go to sleep."

Friday

I awoke to a shriek coming from the bathroom. As I hurried down the hall, Mud Bug came bolting out the bathroom door with what looked like "Alien" type tentacles coming out of her mouth, all moving.

"What the hell?" I blurted out.

Kari poked her head out the bathroom door. "She just came out of the wall with that thing in her mouth. What is it?"

I followed Mud Bug into the kitchen, where whatever she dropped on the floor–something nearly as big as a doorknob–came scurrying toward me. I had no shoes on, so I grabbed the broom out of the kitchen broom closet and whacked it repeatedly until it stopped moving.

At the sound of all this commotion, Kari came naked to the kitchen door and peered in. "Oh yuck! What is it?"

"It's a water bug, I think."

"I don't like it!" Kari explained. "God, I hate this fucking apartment. I hate this whole fucking city!"

Despite the inauspicious beginning, I sailed all the way through Friday, secure in the knowledge that Rick was back and the show was on schedule.

The show went flawlessly. I didn't drink before or during this show because I had to perform on stage–ironically, as a drunk. During our breaks, Rick and I would sit and do crossword puzzles together, sometimes asking each other for help. The audience seemed to like it. Sure, the plot was pointless and convoluted, but it was dazzling to watch and had a Firesign Theatre trippiness to it. When the lights came up, I asked Kari how she liked it, she said, "Weird but fun."

We went out for post-show drinks and let loose. Jim's producer friend from Nickelodeon, a very serious-looking guy named Josh Rosenthal asked me what I wrote. "Most of the stuff about Sea Captain Frank, including the part about his buggering his men."

A grudging smile came on his face. "That was my favorite part," he said. "Listen, Jim and I are doing a skit-oriented show about the trials and tribulations of high school freshmen and we need writers. Are you interested?"

"Can I write from Massachusetts?"

"If you have a phone and a fax, you can write from the moon for all I care," he said. Suddenly, there was life after New York.

At around 2 a.m., Kari and I got out of a taxi in front of our apartment house in Astoria. There was a message on the answering machine. It was Kari's sister's husband. "Hi, it's Mike, your pesky brother-in-law. Listen, the broker called this evening to say they took your offer of one fifty-five. So I just called to say, congratulations. You're broke!"

"Yes!" she exclaimed with her fist in the air, and it drove home to me the fact that this was my last show with Chucklehead.

DEATH CAR TO NEW JERSEY

In my 10 years of living there, New York had failed to mug me, run me down, or throw me in front of an onrushing subway train. The only thing it had successfully done to me was break my heart. Now its cold skeletal claws were reaching up through Connecticut and trying to drag me back down from Boston. I could feel its bony fingers wrapping themselves around me, one by one.

First, Spanky's wedding invitation arrived in my mailbox. I decided to go. Kari decided to stay put. I called Rick and Jack to see if I could stay at their apartment. They said yes and asked how I was getting to New York. I told them I would probably take the train. They asked how I planned on getting to the wedding, which was in Atlantic City. I said I could always drive down. They asked if they could get a ride. I said, yes, of course.

Practically no one I knew in New York, including members of the troupe, owned a car. Cars were more of a liability than an asset because you constantly had to find a place to park it and then constantly move it as the parking laws dictated. But in a small town in Massachusetts, you really needed one. There was a recession going on, I had just spent my life's savings buying a house, I was marginally employed, and Kari had only recently found a job herself, so my parents sold me their old Chevy Citation for a buck. They warned me to drive it sparingly because it already had a hundred and fifty thousand miles on it.

Among people I knew in town, the rusty old Citation was known as the Death Car. The velvet on its ceiling had come free and now dangled down like a shroud on my head as I drove. The shocks were worn out, the car essentially bounced down the highway, and sometimes it felt as if I were trying to steer while suspended in mid-air. It constantly overheated. It drank a quart of oil a week and continually puked it onto the driveway. The oil sometimes drenched the battery and killed it. Sometimes the gas line froze. The damn thing had stranded me on the road three times already and I had only owned it for a couple of years.

Rose called me a day later and asked if she could have a ride, and I said of course. She said she'd meet me at Rick's. Next, Dirk called and asked for a ride. And could I give Judy a ride too? She would rendezvous at his apartment to make things easier for me. And that's how I got roped into driving a whole carload of Chuckleheads into Atlantic City one bleak December morning in a car that spelled certain doom.

The car behaved itself rather well on the trip down, although I found the six-hour drive tiring. But when I started driving down Second Avenue in Manhattan, a strange exhilaration took over me. I went right past Dog Boy Manor, where Spanky and his unemployed actor friends had lived, past 86th Street, where I stayed with a friend when I first moved to New York, past 42nd Street just blocks away from Grand Central Station and East, the sushi bar Kari and I sometimes ate at, past 26th Street, where Rick had once lived, past 25th Street, where I had first lived on arriving in New York, past 14th Street, where Dirk and Russel had lived when they first got to New York, past the East Village and the once-trendy now-passe Sugar Reef, past 6th Street with all its Indian restaurants back to back, where you brought in your own beer; and finally into the Lower East Side, where Rick lived with his lover Jack.

I parked the car across the street from Rick's high-rise apartment building. When I arrived at his penthouse apartment, Rick was resting on the black vinyl couch in front of the TV. He was worn out from his compromised immune system, AIDS medications, smack, methadone, or all four. I glanced out the sliding door to the balcony at the New York skyline, where dozens of sky-scrapers, like stone giants, seemed to huddle together and stare in at us. We had all wanted apartments like this in New York, and I wondered how long Rick would get to enjoy his.

"You're looking well," I tried to say convincingly.

He had open sores all over his neck, arms and legs which, he explained, were from an opportunistic follicle infection. The place smelled of disinfectant. Groggily, he explained where I could safely park my car, and then handed me the keys so I could get back in easily.

I parked the car several blocks away in a large, secluded parking lot not far from the East River. On the way back, I bought a twelve pack, sat down at the TV with Rick, and proceeded with the steady mission of getting hammered. I had just driven six hours through horrendous traffic and I was ready to unwind. Jack arrived and we ordered Chinese food, but I my digestive tract was way, way beyond solid food at this point.

When I awoke on the vinyl sofa, I had a horrendous hang-over. My mouth tasted like bile. The gray fur on my lips told me that one of their twin calicos had spent part of the night on my face. I kept trying to go back to sleep but each time I awoke, I was even more tired than before. Jack ran down to the corner bagel store and brought back bialys. We had coffee and bialys on the living room table, but I was so nauseated I was unable to take more than medicinal amounts of each.

Rose arrived shortly after 9, and we began the death ride in the Death Car at 9:30 a.m. At Dirk's apartment at 86th Street between Amsterdam and Columbus, Jack got out, buzzed Dirk's apartment, and returned to announce that they weren't quite ready yet. Of course not. No one was ever ready. I turned off the ignition and the car sputtered into silence. To keep warm, we huddled in the lobby of Dirk's building.

Ten minutes later, Dirk and Judy came down and we proceeded back to the car. "You've got some rust on the hood," Dirk pointed out, putting his gloved finger on the spot–as well as right through it. "Wow, I'm, like, Superman!"

Dirk slid deftly into the front passenger's seat as if he owned it, while the other four formed a wall of flesh in the back seat. Neither Judy nor Rose had ever bothered to get driver's licenses since they had always lived in New York. Jack had mislaid his license and Rick was just too sick to drive. "Say, Dirk," I asked. "Do you think you might be able to handle some of the driving?"

"Sorry, man. I let my California driver's license expire."

With grim resignation, I put the key in the ignition and turned it. The engine turned over once or twice and died. I tried it again and the same thing happened. "What is it with you and machines, man?" Dirk asked, alluding to the fact that, while the troupe was alive, I had never gotten along with video cameras, microphones, light boards, or anything that ran on electricity. "Way to ruin Spanky's wedding!"

I turned off the engine and just sat there for several moments. I wanted to be gone from that Godforsaken city. There was nothing left for me in it. The troupe had given its last performance, and even the cable TV script work it had engendered had fallen to the wayside. In return for the best 10 years of my life that I had given it, New York had broken my heart, and now I just wanted to be back home in Massachusetts.

"Don't tell me you're giving up!" Jack said.

"No, just giving the battery a rest."

I turned the key and pressed the gas pedal again, and the engine turned over. I kept massaging the gas pedal until, miraculously, the engine sprang back to life. As I pulled out, Dirk looked into my eyes and said, "Say, man, you look like shit. Did you have a couple of martinis for the road or something?"

About 20 minutes into our trek, my neck was already stiff with tension. With the Twin Towers and the rest of the majestic skyline of Manhattan receding in my rearview mirror, Dirk began playing with my visor. I wished he'd cut it out. "What the fuck are you doing?"

"What's this little box with the button, man?"

"That's the garage door opener," I said, as if answering an inquisitive five-year-old.

"Cool!" Dirk said, and pressed the button repeatedly. "Garage door now open." He pressed the button again. "Garage door now closed. Open. Closed. Back in Massachusetts, Kari's probably having a fit." Then he said in a shrieking falsetto: "'Goddamn you Chuckleheads, quit fucking with the garage door opener!'"

The car erupted in shrill laughter. I took a deep breath. Yeah, okay, it was funny. But what I most wanted right now was for all five of the other occupants of the car to sit quietly with their hands folded neatly in front of them. Unfortunately, that just wasn't going to happen.

"Can you turn up the heat? I'm cold," Rick complained.

"Can't. The heater's broken."

"Well, maybe you should get it fixed!"

"Hey, what's with the red light on your dashboard?" Judy asked worriedly.

I looked down at it, wondering if, as I took my eyes off the road, I might swerve across the broken white line and make us collide with an oncoming semi. "That's the 'Service Engine' light," I explained.

"Well, shouldn't you look into it?"

"It's an idiot light. It goes off whenever the odometer hits a certain number of miles. Trust me."

"Are you sure?"

"No," I said. "But do you really want me to stop the fucking car now? We're in danger of being late as it is."

"Yeah, I was going to point that out," said Dirk. "Can't you step on it a little, man?"

I fantasized gripping the steering wheel with my left hand while slapping Dirk silly with my right. As always, the fantasy ended in losing control of the vehicle and killing us all.

The car in front of us was creeping along at just 60 miles an hour. I hit the left turn signal (or "directional" as we called it in Massachusetts) and glided into the left lane. This move was followed by a five-second horn blast. "You just cut that lady off," Rose said. Then she leaned out the window, thumbed her nose at the car behind us, and yelled "Blaaaaah!" In the rearview mirror, I could see the lady throwing up her hands in disbelief.

My stomach shriveled and the blood vessels in my arms constricted as cortisol and epinephrine surged into my bloodstream. My heart pounded uncontrollably, my head was throbbing, and my hands were tingling and trembling uncontrollably. "Listen," I breathed. "Do you mind if I pull over for a couple of seconds?"

"Are you fucking nuts? We're late as it is!" Rick barked. "Why don't you just relax?"

"I'm trying," I said with a cracked voice. "I'm really trying."

I came up to the tollbooth and had a quick decision to make—the "Exact Change" or the "Any Vehicle" lane? The toll was 50 cents. I fished in my pocket and found only one quarter. "Anybody else got a quarter?" I asked.

"A quarter of what?" Rick asked.

"A fucking quarter! Just give me a quarter!"

"Hey, lay off of him. He's had a rough week," Jack protested.

"I think I've got a quarter," Rose said and began rooting through her purse. Quickly, I pulled into the "Exact Change" lane. Rose extended her purse into the front seat and pulled out a myriad items, including lipstick, apartment keys, an aerobics studio schedule, a wind-up plastic robot, a crucifix, some rosary beads, a Pez dispenser, a tampon, some hair thingies, and a small bottle of aspirin. The way she was going, I expected her to pull out a series of tied-together brightly colored scarves and a dove.

Meanwhile, the car ahead of me had gone and I slowly inched my way up to the change receptacle. "Well?" I asked. A tsunami of sound broke over us as the driver behind me leaned on his horn for a good 10 seconds. Now I felt as if someone were dribbling a basketball inside my chest. Rick rolled down his window, poked his head out, and gave the guy the finger. In the rearview mirror, I looked back at the other driver, whose swearing was drowned out by another long wail of his car horn.

Rose finally removed everything from her purse, turned it over, and began to shake it. I couldn't tell if this were all some insidiously evil comedy act, or whether she was really that slow and ineffectual. Suddenly, I hated her.

Finally, with a deadpan expression, she opened a tiny change purse and handed me a quarter. I tossed the two quarters into the pot and floored the gas pedal. A censuring buzzer sounded from within the tollbooth.

"Hey, man, you don't have the green light," Dirk pointed out.

I slammed on the brakes and the horn behind me blared instantaneously, as if it were directly wired to my brake pedal. My heart pounded so explosively I was afraid it would break open my sternum. "Fuck you, you fucking asshole!" I said to no one in particular.

"Just go, man. The light's green *now*," Dirk said.

Except that I couldn't. The car had died. I threw it into "Park" again, turned the ignition, and began pumping. It turned over once and died. The car behind me blasted the horn, the car behind him joined in, and soon the whole lane erupted into a Stravinsky concert. Trembling, I turned the key again and pumped. The engine started. I shifted into "Drive," and stomped on the gas pedal, and the car screeched forward with a jolt.

"Take it easy, Rob. You're making Rick carsick," Jack said.

"You're all going to fucking die!" I muttered.

"What'd you say?" Dirk asked.

"Never mind."

I started to imagine the crash. I imagined passing out from an anxiety attack and losing control of the car, the car going over a guard rail and then flipping over multiple times. Just before the car landed, upside down, at the bottom of a rocky culvert, crushing us all, I hoped I would have time to scream, "See what you made me do?"

Because there were six of us and we were part of the same troupe, we would have a single funeral and it would be quite large. The surviving Chuckleheads would reminisce about the dead Chuckleheads, about the tragedy of such wonderful, talented young people cut down in their prime and about the sad irony of it happening on their way to a wedding. For a moment, I imagined a New York Post front-page headline blaring something like, "Nothing Funny About Carload of Dead Clowns," but the sad truth was we just weren't famous enough for a front-page tabloid headline and never had been.

I was starting to wonder if the "Check Engine" light might actually mean something. I had noticed that whenever I tried to accelerate, the Citation was very slow to respond, and every so often it seemed to slow down for reasons of its own. I began to suspect that one of the cylinders was misfiring, and wondered how long I could get by on three cylinders. I was relieved when the exit for Atlantic City came up.

I had never been to Atlantic City, but it was as depressing as I had always imagined. The sky was gray, the streets were now washed out and virtually deserted, and once bright casino signs now looked dingy and eaten up by ocean air. "Take a left up here," said Rose, holding the directions.

"No, right," said Judy, craning her neck over the directions.

"Which is it?"

"Right."

"No, left."

I made the snap judgment that, being a writer rather than an actress, Judy was the smarter of the two females, and started to go left, until I saw a "One Way Do Not Enter" sign. I backed up, eliciting another horn blast, and turned right. Our hotel was there on the right.

As I pulled into the driveway, a valet came up, opened the door, and said, "I'll take it from here." My Guardian Angel.

It was 11:15. We had exactly 15 minutes till the wedding started. As the valet slid into the driver's seat, we grabbed our bags out of the back hatch. I pulled my wallet out of my pocket, dropped it on the pavement, picked it up, pulled out a couple of bills, and handed them to the valet. As we gathered at the registration desk, Dirk said, "We'll rendezvous here in ten minutes."

Fortunately, registration went very fast. I rushed into my room, pulled off my shoes, jeans, and shirt. I threw on my white shirt, quickly tied my tie around it, found it uneven, loosened it, and retied it again. I unzipped my suit bag, took out my suit, threw on my jacket, threw on my pants, and threw on my shoes. I fished my wallet and hotel key out of my jeans and stuffed them into my suit pants. I looked at my watch. It was 11:25.

When I got to the registration desk, none of the Chuckleheads were there. The clerk at the registration desk pointed me out one of the side doors. I rushed out the door onto the boardwalk, to see Rick and Jack, now in suits, disappearing around the corner of the building. When I turned that corner, I saw my five friends sprinting down the street, the girls' high heels clacking noisily against the pavement.

The church, which was a block away, was dark, gaudy, and imposing. All around, there were tortured stained-glass angels dimmed by the overcast skies behind them. In gold mosaic tiles, Jesus, nailed and bleeding all over the cross, was weeping in physical and emotional agony. We hurried down the aisle and took our places on the heavy wooden pews. I looked around and saw a few familiar faces, such as Jim, Angie, Peter, and Spanky's brother, but the rest were total strangers.

The grim ritual started with funereal wedding music. A sweet-looking lady I had never seen before, dressed in a wedding gown, was escorted down the aisle. Word had it that she was from a wealthy, ultra-religious Italian family that was quite prominent in Atlantic City. Spanky, dwarfed in a big and expensive suit, was escorted down the aisle by his friend Dave. And thus began one of the longest weddings I had ever attended.

Chapters and verses were quoted. Solemn and terrible vows were made, seemingly under penalty of death. Arcane blessings were said in Latin. Plenty of grave symbolic rituals were performed using sacred objects. I was waiting for the part where they cut off Spanky's pinky and threw it into a cauldron of fire.

The anxiety had never totally left me. My neck was still stiff, my heart was pounding, the mausoleum air was suffocating me, and my tie seemed to be getting tighter and tighter around my neck.

At one point, for reasons that weren't completely apparent to me, we were all kneeling on little padded structures apparently designed for just that purpose. I glanced up at the tortured face of Christ, whose suffering completely overshadowed my own puny mortal thoughts that day. He seemed to be saying: "Having a bad day? I'll show you a bad day!"

On the other side of Rick and Jack, Rose was snickering, her face turning nearly as red as her hair. Watching her, Dirk started snickering too. Judy looked at them with disapproval, but her mouth was already beginning to tremble. Now Rick and Jack were snickering. I bumped shoulders with Rick and asked him what was so funny. "I'll tell you later," he whispered.

Rose took a deep breath and adopted a solemn and innocent affect. Dirk wiped the grin off his face, Judy shut her eyes and grimaced, and Rick and Jack bowed their heads in abject submission. Seconds later, Rick's abdomen went into a weird kind of spasm, his face turned redder and redder, and tears welled up in his eyes. Finally he gasped for air and began laughing out loud again. Soon all five of them were hunkered down on the kneeling pads, snickering hysterically and trying to hide as people on all sides of us started to glare. I half expected some gorillas in expensive suits to escort us outside and teach us some respect.

That's when all the inner demons that had been welling up inside me for the past two hours spewed forth from my mouth in a loud guffaw that made strangers kneeling in front of us turn and stare. I writhed on the floor with the rest of them, wheezing and wiping tears from my eyes, trying desperately not to disrupt our dear friend's austere wedding. As I kneeled there, succumbing to the laughter, all my panic left me.

I never did find out what was so funny. But the truth is it just didn't matter.

ROB DINSMOOR

CHUCKLEHEAD
GOES TO HOLLYWOOD:
GET THE REAL STORY HERE!

The following excerpts are reprinted with permission from The Special Hollywood Wedding Issue (Fall 1995) of the Rob & Kari Newsletter ("for people who care what happens to Rob and Kari"). Yet, this candied-ass piece of tabloid journalism clearly glosses over the important scenes behind the scenes of this important Chucklehead event. Now the truth can be told!

Jim and Angie Wed; Earthquake Ensues

(WEST HOLLYWOOD, CA) – Chucklehead couple Jim Jones and Angie Sardinia were wed Saturday June 24 at Saint Anthony's church. The church did not tumble to the ground, as some had predicted, but an earthquake hit the area two days later.

One quiet Saturday morning in May, Rob received something in the mail that made his jaw gape and his head spin. "What is it?" Kari asked, alarmed by his expression. It was an envelope addressed in calligraphy from Los Angeles, and it could only mean one thing: Hell had frozen over, i.e., Jim and Angie were finally getting married.

"Well, I'll be a son of a bitch. The Battlin' Jonses did it. They really went and did it," I muttered, showing the invitation to Kari. "What do you think?"

"Of course we're going. You kidding?"

We immediately took a telephone survey of who was going. It looked like Dirk, Rose, and Pat would be able to make it. Peter had family obligations. Judy's mother was having her fiftieth birthday. Spanky couldn't afford it. With Rick's medical expenses,

Rick and Jack couldn't afford it. "We could pay for your plane tickets. That would be our wedding present to Jim and Angie," Kari said to Jack, much to my surprise.

Actually, for once, something like wasn't totally out of the question. After four years of scraping by, things had started to turn around. The recession was over, its fallout was gone, Kari was working for a consulting firm that made more money than it knew what to do with, and I was now flush with medical writing clients.

"Well, it's not just that. Honestly, I don't think Rick could handle the plane ride," Jack explained.

The last I'd heard of Jim and Angie, they had bought a nice little stucco bungalow in West Hollywood and had enough scratch to hire Mexican servants. Jim was head writer for one of my favorite cartoon shows and had tried unsuccessfully to sell some of my pitches. Now he was producing animated segments for Nickelodeon in his garage, kitchen, back yard, and bathroom using toy action figures. Angie was taking small roles in films and working as an extra in workout videos. Word had it she was still so buff you could bounce a quarter off her butt.

Rob and Kari flew into L.A. on Friday afternoon and checked into the Beverly-Laurel Motor Hotel, which was the most economical of all the hotels Angie had suggested. Many exterior shots for the series "Ellen" are taken around there. The Beverly-Laurel offers a free postcard depicting the hotel surrounded by famous landmarks. The motel is portrayed as being somewhat larger than the Hollywood Bowl and the La Brea Tar Pits, but with a disclaimer on the bottom line that says, "Not Drawn to Scale."

At Jim and Angie's barbecue that night, they met an assortment of Sardinias, Jonses, L.A. actors and writers, people from Nickelodeon (Roseanne Fiatarone, Josh Rosenthal), Chuckleheads (Pat, Rose, and Dirk), and various other people doing unspeakable things (i.e., they didn't want to talk about them).

On our way from the Beverly-Laurel Motor Lodge, Kari

and I stopped off to get a sixpack and a couple of Zimas, and then found Jim and Angie's address. Even though I had never been to West Hollywood, the neighborhood looked vaguely familiar: I had probably seen it in at least one episode of "Dragnet" and possibly even some Laurel and Hardy comedies.

In the back yard, someone I didn't know was guarding the grill and spread over the back yard were about a dozen other people I didn't know. Slowly, I started to recognize remotely familiar people, faces from Nickelodeon, including Jim's co-producer on one of the shows I used to write for. Same smart but irritable face, same thinning hair, same dark eyebrows that hung over glasses shielding those piercing eyes. Except instead of sitting behind a cramped desk in a windowless office, he was wearing a polo shirt and soaking up rays. "Josh!" I said, enthusiastically, and stepped up to shake his hand.

His smile was not completely convincing and his eyes narrowed warily. "Rob, how are you?"

"Great. What have you been up to?" I asked, and his eyes narrowed with downright suspicion.

He looked off in the distance and took a drink from his diet coke. "You know, a little writing, a little producing. Kind of dabbling in a little of this and a little of that. You know how it is."

"Nickelodeon stuff?"

"No. Well, yeah, a little, but not really," he said, and clenched his jaw tightly. "How about you?"

"Oh, you know, medical stuff," I said. "Pays the bills."

"Roseanna!" he called out to a woman I recognized, a director on one of the shows I'd worked for on Nickelodeon while I was still in New York. He tried to make a beeline for her but she was instantly in our little group, thus foiling Josh's apparent escape plan. She gave him a hug and then smiled and waved at me, recognizing me without really being able to pin down who I was. "I haven't seen you in ages!" Josh said to her.

"I'm out of L.A. now," she explained. "I'm writing as well as producing now–I never realized how tough it was!"

"Really? What kind of writing are you doing?" I asked.

"Whatever they'll pay me to do!" she said, shaking her head, laughing, and showing her toothy, girlish grin.

"Listen, I have some stuff I need to talk to you about," Josh told her, his pupils fixed on hers like a laser beam.

"I'm all ears!" she said.

"This isn't a good time," he said, winking at her. "Later."

I was pissed. I had asked perfectly reasonable, pleasant questions. I was not here to network, I had never pushed my talent on anyone, but suddenly I felt like I was some guy selling time shares at a funeral or something. It was yet another reminder that the people I used to work with had shut me off and my comedy writing career was over.

"Nice seeing you both again," I said, and returned to Kari's side.

Just then, Dirk showed up in a cool, very expensive-looking white suit. I shook his hand and Kari pecked him on the cheek. "You look great!" she said to him. "What have you been up to?"

"Nothing very interesting."

When Pat arrived on the scene, Josh Rosenthal's wife gestured toward him and said, "That's the guy from the plane! I'm sure of it!" to which Josh replied, "You're crazy! That's not him!" It turns out they had sat next to Pat on a flight from Newark and had accidentally startled him from his nap by lifting the window blind. All was forgiven but karma reigned: Josh later became ill and now suspects it was the chicken.

Kari took an instant liking to Pat, whom she had previously avoided meeting because of scary stories about him, the warrior babe poster catalogues he publishes, and his final Chucklehead appearance, in "Why I Quit Chucklehead." During the evening, Pat paid the bride a compliment, declaring, "You could bounce a quarter off her butt!"

Photo Caption: Rob "going LA," wears his first collarless shirt.

Photo Caption: Kari, not accustomed to LA etiquette, shows up wearing nylons—and a sunburn.

At the wedding, the Chuckleheads were on good behavior. They did not start making each other giggle uncontrollably, as they had done at Spanky's wedding. In fact, Pat, Rose, and Kari quietly muttered all those things that good Catholics are supposed to mutter at wedding services, which Protestants and Jews cannot quite hear or understand.

However, others were not so well mannered. The priest brought the house down by mistakenly referring to Angie as "Jennifer," but then unsuccessfully tried to milk the joke repeatedly in his monologue. And Maggie Wilcox, whom we believe to be Episcopalian, went up front for a communion wafer, later explaining that she hadn't eaten all day.

When the wedding let out around 2 p.m., Pat was relieved that no lightening had struck and the church had not collapsed. However, someone pointed out to Angie that there was still more than an hour before the reception started, and she advised her guests in her favorite Yenta voice, to "talk amongst yourselves."

To kill time, Pat drove Rob, Kari, Maggie, and his friend Irene around in Irene's car, while Irene pointed out historical spots, such as where Janis Joplin overdosed and where Sal Mineo was stabbed to death. They also saw the Walk of Stars, Grummond's Chinese Theater, the Guiness Museum, the Ripley's Believe It Or Not Museum, and the Church of Scientology.

The reception was held at the gorgeous Wattles Mansion up in the Hollywood hills, which has beautiful gardens and a stunning view of Los Angeles. It was such a warm, pleasant, funny, and relaxing experience, we're honestly at a loss to find bad things to say about it.

The sun was blazing overhead and seemed to be fixed in place, and the afternoon seemed to be lasting forever. Kari and I were floating from table to table, eating great appetizers and seafood, toasting the bride and groom, looking at photos of Rose's cats, and catching up on Pat's smut business. Yet, throughout the course of the afternoon, the distinction between old friends and strangers began to blur, and we found ourselves talking comfortably and intimately with people we hadn't known before.

Even though these weren't top Hollywood celebrities, everyone was in the Biz. And a huge percentage of even the wanna-be actors were physically stunning and unusually charming. I didn't get irate when some polished Latino lothario was flirting with Kari and making her giggle because, meanwhile, his darkly sensual and stunningly dressed Latina wife was batting her eyes at me and asking me about the plays that I had written. And soon another voluptuous woman with a very low décolletage and a very mysterious chasm between her breasts was wrapping her hands around my upper arm, and saying, "I hear you're one of the Chucklehead writers. What else have you done?" The thought that I might somehow be of use to any of these women was exciting to me.

Meanwhile, Kari was passing business cards to me, with the name of some of my plays on the back, and winking. Left and right, we were flirting and trading contact with the Beautiful People and the fact that it would almost certainly come to naught was just about beside the fact. We were playing the game. We were in the Olympian playground of Eros and Aphrodite, where satyrs and sirens went to cavort and play, and we were among them!

At one point, Dirk had removed his jacket and was running all over the lawn, throwing the Frisbee, tackling the Frisbee to the ground, and generally working up a serious sweat. Then he sat down at one of the picnic tables beside me and across from Pat. Pat rolled his eyes because he still fostered a deep-abiding grudge against Dirk after all these years: "Fucking Dirk. He's at his best friend's wedding and he has to roll around in the mud and get completely sweaty."

I stuck my nose in the air, looked around and said, "Gosh, are we near the ocean?" Then I looked over at Dirk and said, "Oh." Everyone at the table laughed, except Dirk, and I had just scored a direct hit. And life was good.

Photo Caption: Dirk, drenched in sweat after a Frisbee game on the lawn, stands upwind of the bride (left) and shares a beer—and his own bodily secretions—with the groom (right).

Photo caption: Group photo of some of the now-defunct Chuckleheads and their groupies.

Photo caption: Man and wife.

The shadows had started to get a little longer, and the air temperature had dropped down from about 80 to 70 degrees. "You know what I think would be a great wedding gift?" Kari suggested. "A phone call to Rick."

And so I found a nice, quiet pay phone in the lobby of the Mansion, while Pat went to find Angie. Charging the call on my credit card, I dialed the number of Rick and Jack's apartment. Part of me wanted to get no answer because things could get, well, emotional.

"Hello."

"Hello, Jack?:

"Yeah."

"It's Rob."

"Hi!"

"Hi, we're calling from Angie's wedding."

"Cool. Wish we could be there. How is it?"

"Really nice. We were thinking. It might be nice if we could all talk to Rick. Since you guys couldn't make it. If he's up to it. "

"Yeah. I'll see."

A few moments later, I heard a weak, sleepy voice. "Hello?"

"Rick. It's Rob!"

"Who?" he asked, and I couldn't tell whether he was just very sleepy or all drugged up.

"Rob. I'm calling from Angie's wedding." Dead silence on the other end. "Are you okay? You sound a little drugged up and confused." Silence. "We're all having a great time, but we miss you." Incomprehensible muttering. "What was that you said?" Silence. "Okay. Good talking to you. I'm going to pass you on to Kari now."

Kari took the phone and said "Hi, sweetie! It's Kari!" I could tell from the way she was talking to him, and the way she kept repeating herself, that he hadn't gotten much more coherent, but she was engaging him more than I had.

By the time she got off the phone, word had gotten to all of the Chuckleheads there and all of them—except Angie—were standing in a circle around us.

"I couldn't find Angie. Has anybody seen her?" Pat asked.

"No," Dirk responded, "But I've been telling everybody to pass the word to her."

Kari handed Rick over to Rose. "Hi, honey! That's right. It's Rose. Not feeling that good, huh? I'm sorry." Rose switched ears, cradled the phone on her shoulder, and gently rocked back and forth. "Oh, honey, I wish I could be there to make you feel better!"

A very disturbing image embedded itself in my mind and wouldn't go away. I pictured Rick, helplessly encased inside the plastic telephone receiver, and we could only pass him around between us and talk to him through these little holes in the plastic. The image really started to bother me, and emotionally I felt myself tumbling down some kind of deep, dark abyss. "I feel really weird and out of sorts right now," I told Kari. "I think I'm having one of my anxiety attacks."

"It's called *sadness*. You're sad," she said. "And it's perfectly okay and normal to feel that way, so don't fight it."

Angie stormed into the room, wedding gown wafting behind her. She looked at Rose with what bordered on alarm. "Is that Rick?"

Rose nodded. "Guess what, baby! Angie's here and she wants to talk to you!" she cooed over the phone.

And so she handed Rick over to Angie, tenderly laying the

receiver in Angie's hands as if it were a premature newborn, and saying, "I should warn you–he's a little woozie."

Even before she lifted the phone to her mouth, she was crying. "Hi, honey!" she sobbed. I was tumbling head-first down that emotional abyss, which seemed to have no bottom whatsoever. Angie's wedding radiance was gone and now her mascara was running, her eyes were deep red, and her cheeks were all swollen and puffy. Finally she couldn't talk any more, and handed Rick over to Dirk, who said "How are you, big guy?" I could hear deep, inconsolable wailing from the earpiece. Sobbing uncontrollably, Angie went into the ladies room, followed by Rose, calling out, "You okay, honey?"

I had finally landed per force at the bottom of the abyss, and that bottom was the realization that I had single-handedly ruined Angie's wedding day. I began to hyperventilate. Kari gently stroked my back. "Listen, kiddo. It's okay. Really. Calling Rick was a *good* thing."

I excused myself and went into the men's bathroom. I was thankful that no one was there. For about five minutes, I cried as quietly as I could and then climbed back out of the abyss, into the sunshine.

Rob and Kari awoke at 5:30 a.m. on Sunday morning. The Filipino desk clerk explained that the taxis weren't running till 8 o'clock but offered to drive them himself–for a fee. After the driver got somewhat lost, Rob and Kari barely caught their 8 a.m. flight and arrived in South Hamilton, exhausted, at about 6:30 p.m. An earthquake registering 4.9 on the Richter scale hit L.A. around 2 a.m. Monday morning, exactly 36 hours too late.

ROB DINSMOOR

THE TOUGHEST AUDIENCE

I think I was on the Lower East Side, not far from his apartment, when I saw Rick. It was probably winter, because everyone was bundled up and everything was gray. I saw him across the street, walking quickly, looking distracted. "Hey, Rick!" I called out. "Wait up!"

He looked up at me and smiled, but continued walking. What was wrong with him? Where was he going in such a hurry? I started walking in the same direction. "When did you get out of the hospital?" I shouted. Again, he looked over and smiled, but his pace never faltered. "You know, you had us all really worried! I mean, your liver shut down, your kidneys had shut down, you were on dialysis, you were on a respirator! To be quite honest, you were a total mess! We really didn't know if you'd make it!"

I was having trouble keeping up with him, even keeping him in sight. He kept disappearing behind the throngs of faceless people passing by in long coats. Every time I tried to cross the street, there would be a procession of cars with their headlights on. "Rick! Wait up! Are you mad at me? I know I haven't been around much since we moved away. Are we still friends?"

He turned another corner and was gone. Just then, Kari shook me awake. "Get up. We have to get dressed soon," she said.

We were in a strange place that I soon recognized as my friend Kim's apartment in New York. It took me a few moments to realize why I was there: Rick's funeral.

After hearing the news of Rick's demise, Kari and I had arranged to fly down to New York Friday. I asked my friend Kim if we could stay in her apartment on Second Avenue. She would be out of town but said we could stay there and FedExed us her spare keys.

The funeral was arranged for Sunday morning. Friday night, there was an informal gathering at Jack's apartment. The apartment that Jack and Rick had shared was on the twentieth floor of a high-rise, and the view off the terrace was literally breathtaking. From that height, the southern end of Manhattan, with all its towers and streets and expressways and bridges, looked like a giant, intricate mechanical toy. And sitting on that terrace, especially at sunset, was like having balcony seats to the grand spectacle that was New York.

Jack pretty much stayed in the bedroom most of the night, occasionally visited by the Catholic funeral matrons in our midst: Spanky's wife Maria brought salad, garlic bread, and lasagna, and she and Angie, Rose, and Kari took care of all the petty arrangements, worked as liaisons between Jack and the party, and generally smoothed over all the social bumps, all with these warm smiles on their faces. These women all seemed to feel at home around death, and they flitted around Jack's apartment as if preparing for a baby shower rather than a funeral service.

I myself was not ready to see Jack. If he had looked into my eyes, he would not have gotten the warm, spiritual vibes the Catholic funeral matrons put out. He would have seen the unspeakable horror, the overwhelming sadness, and the frigid emptiness inside me. I was a ghost. Although I ridiculed the very idea of death in much of my writing and had done practically everything I could think of to hasten its arrival, the truth was that I wasn't ready to look death in the face. My eyes would have said, "Jesus, Jack, this is so awful I can't even stand to look at you! All I see when I look at you is death! Rick's dead! We're all going to die, all of us! I don't want to die!"

I, Ghost Boy, moved along the periphery of the troupe, soaking up pockets of warmth and light wherever I could find them. We did what we usually did—hung out, drank, smoked, and gabbed. "Last year when Rick was in the hospital and not doing so well, Dirk told him to hurry up and get well because Chucklehead was getting back together again," Spanky told me.

"That's not true!" Dirk broke in. "I mean, it was a joke and he knew it!"

"I don't want to sound weird, but the moment of death was really sweet," Angie said to me in an offhand way. "His vital signs were falling apart, and he knew he was about to die. And then we all joined hands in a circle around him and chanted. And then he sighed and then he was gone. When I go, I want to go like that. You should have been there."

She did not mean it to be an accusation, but that's how I took it. I probably could have been there at his death bed, but it would have meant taking the Death Train down to the horrific soul-eating chaos that was New York, visiting St. Luke's House of Death, and coming face-to-face with Death Boy and his entourage. At the time of Rick's death, I was sitting in an empty house up in Massachusetts, where I got a collect call from Judy at a pay phone. She didn't need to tell me the reason for her call, but she did anyway: "I really hate to have to tell you this way, but Rick's gone," she said. "I just thought you'd want to know."

I had wondered whether Paul was going to put together a "Greatest Hits of Rick" compilation, but he didn't, and I doubt anyone would have felt like watching it anyway. At least not right now.

If they had made a TV documentary on him, they would have used a video of that really, really weird sketch he was in where he played this pathetic, lugubrious lounge singer named Frankie Nay who really wanted to be a clown. At the end of the skit, he's in full clown regalia, singing this bittersweet song about his giant pantaloons. I was pretty sure Paul never got that one on tape. For some reason, just remembering that skit disturbed me.

The party ended when Maria came out of the bedroom

and quietly told us all that Jack was really tired and it was time for us to leave.

Saturday, I wanted to try to get together with some of my non-Chucklehead friends, like my former boss Erika and my childhood friend Dave, but Kari insisted that we should get together with the troupe. "Surely, people are planning to get together tonight somewhere," she said. So we bagged plans to visit other people and I left messages on everyone's answering machine that "it would be nice to get together" and "please call" and gave them Kim's number.

Then we watched great films from Kim's video collection. My tastes normally ran to the horrific, like "Aliens," "The Exorcist," and "Rosemary's Baby." That afternoon, however, I couldn't even watch a rerun of "Gilligan's Island" because I couldn't face the grim reality that all seven castaways would probably die on that island, one at a time, and that the last survivor would probably kill himself to escape the excruciating loneliness. We wound up watched lush life-affirming films like "Eat Drink Man Woman" and "The Scent of Green Papaya" while we waited for someone, anyone, to return our call. No one did.

When dinnertime rolled around, I wanted to go out to eat, but Kari was worried that we'd miss a call, so we ordered Chinese food to be delivered and I made a trip down to the deli next door for beer. No one called us back. Kari was worried that, somewhere, all the Chuckleheads were getting together and crying and hugging and generally having a great cathartic time, and the two of us were out of the loop.

Sunday morning, on awakening from my sad dream, I had mixed feelings about attending the service. On the one hand, it would be comforting to be around other people, but I was dreading the thought of having to talk about Rick in front of a crowd of people.

I had never seen the Chuckleheads so nicely dressed as they were at the service, which was held in a tight little funeral home in the Village. "I half expected Dirk to show up in that cheesy brown suit of his," Rose remarked. I knew the one she meant. He'd worn it for years whenever he wanted to play uptight, middle-class, middle-management types, but for years he had transported it in garbage bags and duffel bags and it was now terminally wrinkled. In fact, Dirk now earned big bucks writing for TV and actually wore a nice, pressed suit to the service.

It was then I noticed that some of us had visibly aged since the troupe disbanded and some of us hadn't. Dirk was no longer the surfer dude. Years of having a grown-up job for grown-up money had thinned his hair a little and his face looked thinner. Maria had apparently kept Spanky well fed and he now had touches of gray on his temples. Pat had gained back all the weight he had valiantly lost in the early days of Chucklehead, and now he just looked tired. Jim, tanned and dressed hip, with a pony tail and big circles under his eyes, looked like an aging Hollywood rock star. Somehow, Angie, Rose, Peter, Judy, and I seemed to have dodged the bullet so far.

Some comforting old and new faces shown up. Peter had brought his two-year-old son Kyle, who was taking some of his first steps as an erect human being.

Rose's ex-boyfriend, Remy, was there. I hadn't seen him in five years. He was in his mid forties now and looked even more distinguished. His golden hair and mustache now had a gray tint to them, and when I gave him a hug, there was something very reassuring in his fine graying stubble brushing against my cheek.

Russell was there, and looked pretty much the same. He, too, was married and had a baby daughter at home. "I really like being a daddy," he told Angie and Rose. Then a gushy smile flickered across his face, and then he looked self-conscious at having gone gushy.

In addition to Jack and the troupe, there were about twenty men and women seated in the rear, all seemingly in their seventies. When I looked at them quizzically, Maria said simply, "Family."

"Jack's family or Rick's?"

"I don't know," Maria said. "But that's his father over there."

I had never met Rick's father. Though in his late sixties, he was impeccably dressed and his nails were well manicured and he looked like an advertising executive. He was having a private conversation with Angie, hugging her in what I thought to be a not entirely appropriate manner. After all, his son was in a box in the front of the room. Rick's mother wasn't there either, though I didn't expect her: In the final years, the only contact Rick had with her was through their respective lawyers, generally having to do who was trying to do what with his grandfather's estate.

"You should go say hi," Kari said.

I stepped up to him and gently patted him on the shoulder. He turned with what looked like great irritation. "Hi, Mr. Ratner, I'm Rob. I just wanted to let you know how sad I was to hear about Rick. He was my best friend in the troupe."

Rick's dad nodded at me and then kept staring at me in a way that suggested he wanted me to go away, so I did.

We all sat down in folding metal chairs. The funeral director quietly moved to the front of the room and explained that, at Jack's request, people could come up front and share their memories of Rick. As I thought about what I was going to say, I was hit with a barrage of Rick flashbacks:

• He would frequently hold the script meetings at his studio apartment on 26th Street. The place was booby-trapped: Bookshelves mounted tenuously on his walls. Remote controls for his TV, VCR, and stereo all over the floor. Rickety furniture. Prized record albums just standing up loosely, leaning against each other, against the wall. One time, clumsy after a few beers, I brushed against his record albums, sending them toppling forward. Distracted by that, I stepped on one of his remotes. "Just sit down!" he said, shoving me toward the couch. I landed heavily, and the legs of his couch broke. Rick shrieked.

• During rehearsals, Rick would sometimes grab the mike and do the "M-m-m-mom" rap that everyone loved. He lyrics all had to do with child abuse and neglect and were punctuated with, "M-m-m-mom!"

• After I moved to Astoria and Kari moved in with me, we frequently hosted Chucklehead dinners of Thai food. In the midst of the party, I came into the bedroom to see our Calico cat, Mud Bug, up on the ironing board. Rick, cigarette cocked rakishly in his mouth, was ironing her. What he didn't realize was that the iron was actually on and Mud Bug's fur was very, very warm. She didn't seem to be in any distress, but Rick felt horrible about it.

• One afternoon, we met to go see Wim Wenders' "Wings of Desire," which had just come out. It had gotten rave reviews. I had had four beers before seeing it, and I'm pretty sure Rick was on heroin that day. Half an hour into the picture, with its bleak, brooding, black-and-white landscape, I was bored to tears. At one point, as the music laboriously returned and the grim angel launched into another round of poetry, I began snickering uncontrollably. Then Rick started laughing at my plight, and soon many of the audience members around us were laughing, too. We lasted through the entire thing. As we were taking a leak afterward, still laughing, I asked him, "So what did you think of it?" Rick answered: "I thought it was derivative of 'Lady and the Tramp.'" Then two other guys in the men's room started laughing, too.

• One afternoon, Rick showed Kari and me a video of a low-budget action film he had acted in called "Search and Destroy." Depicting a germ warfare disaster in a small town that made all the townspeople turn homicidal, it was one of those productions where they had filmed the action-packed movie trailer first, in order to get backers, before shooting the entire thing. Rick had something like six roles in it. Due in part to cast member no-shows, the director cast Rick as at least one national guardsman (wearing a gas mask), a lab technician, at least one redneck (in a pick-up truck at night), and a truck driver in a diner who says, "How's the chicken, Flo?" Spanky had a small role as a spectacled waiter who hangs himself, and there was a quick cameo of our friend Dave Weber throwing up. Rick was wonderfully versatile in it and I was actually quite proud of him.

• Rick had always moved from one waitering job to another, and spent whatever he made on movies, videos, laser discs and drugs. Finally, his level of debt got so bad his father convinced him to declare bankruptcy. Although Kari and I were happy for him, it bothered us that it would so easy for him to start over. When we prepared to move into our new house in Massachusetts, we were touched that he bought us a portable phone as a housewarming gift—until we realized he had charged it to his credit card just two days before declaring bankruptcy and he had no intention of paying for it.

Though essentially sweet and fun, he could always be a tad difficult, and became more so once he was diagnosed with AIDS. After Kari and I had moved to Massachusetts, Rick and Jack frequently invited us down for weekends. Rick loved our visits and the special attention we lavished on him. We took turns posing for pictures with Rick, who was now pale, puffy, scabby, unshaven, and losing his hair. Sometimes he would stay in bed most of the weekend, suffering from anxiety attacks from heroin withdrawal (which was prolonged since he continually managed to get his hands on the stuff from time to time) or from the effects of the methadone or the various AIDS drugs.

One Saturday, he was going on and on about an episode of "The Outer Limits" written by Harlan Ellison that we absolutely had to see. He had a book that outlined episodes of "The Outer Limits" and described it in glowing terms. I was looking forward to it. About five minutes into the episode, Rick looked in the TV Guide to discover that "Howard Stern" was on. He switched channels and we began watching "Homeless Hollywood Squares" in which the contestants were actual homeless people and some of the "stars" were mentally ill. Kari and I both hated it with a passion and were disturbed that Rick found it funny. Despite my pleading, Rick insisted on taping "Howard Stern" and I realized I would never get to see the famous Harlan Ellison episode of "The Outer Limits."

In the middle of "Howard Stern," the phone rang and Rick pressed the "mute" button. He and Jack were invited to a party hosted by the Gay Men's Health Crisis, and they left us watching a TV show we hated, because I couldn't figure out Rick's complicated system of three remote control units. At one point, he called to ask if we were having a good time. When he hung up, very abruptly it seemed to me, I drove my fist into the concrete wall of his terrace, making my knuckles swell and bleed. I never mentioned it to them, because I didn't want to cause Rick any undue stress.

On some of my later visits, Rick and I would sit out on their wondrous terrace, drinking and talking about the meaning of life. The terrace was decorated with thousands of distinct lights from the hundreds of skyscrapers around us, and we were serenaded by a symphony of distant shouts, rumbling trains, horns, and sirens. Rick was on multiple medications, including methadone for his heroin addiction, and tended to nod off with a cigarette in his hand. It was my job to pick up the lit cigarettes as he dropped them. If he was sufficiently conscious, I would hand them back to him and light them.

Lately, I had been having a difficult time dealing emotionally with all the death and dying around me, including Rick's. I tried reading Sogyal Rinpoche's *The Tibetan Book of the Living and Dying*, a sort of primer on Tibetan Buddhism. It almost had me convinced that I could inhale all the suffering and horrible shit going on in Rick's body and then exhale it harmlessly into the air in a plume of oily black smoke. I tried it a few times and nothing happened. I started to have my doubts about Tibetan Buddhism. After all, Dirk frequently went on spiritual hiatus in Tibet and came back the same asshole he was when he left. (Or maybe he was trying to evolve into a *perfect asshole*.)

For the last year of his life, Rick was in and out of the intensive care unit. I frequently called him up, only to find him too spaced out to talk. Sometimes I had to tell him I couldn't understand a word he was saying and should probably sign off. One time I couldn't hear him because of the noise of the respirator. "I can't turn it off, because I'd die," he explained.

The last time I called him, he screamed at me as he answered the phone: "Motherfucker! Your timing is incredible! I'm having the worst goddamn case of diarrhea, and when the phone rang, it made me tip over my bedpan! I'm sitting here in my own shit thanks to you!" I apologized and, after that, quit calling.

Dirk was the first one to share his memories, giving a very eloquent speech about Rick and how he lived life to the fullest. How he was never afraid to do anything for the troupe, no matter how dangerous or humiliating. "And even though that horrible disease ravaged his lungs, his liver, and his kidneys, there's one organ it left intact—his heart. Because Rick had the biggest, strongest heart of anyone I know."

Angie and Rose both spoke of the close friendship they

had formed with Rick, how he read voraciously, and how he exposed them to some of the best—and worst—books they'd ever read.

I looked back at the septuagenarians to see how they were reacting. They weren't. Again, I wondered who they were.

Next, Spanky got up to the podium, his eyes tearing over. Except for the gray hairs nipping at his temples, he would have looked like a high school kid wearing his first grown-up suit. The jacket, tie, and shirt were all blended together so tastefully, I was sure Maria had picked it out for him. "I'm here to tell you I just lost my best friend," he said. "I had just moved here from San Francisco and I met him at the Neighborhood Group Theater. He was a better actor than I am. He got all the good roles and I didn't. I was jealous about it at the time. But I shouldn't have been. He would never miss an opportunity to do something good for you.

"Right after I got here, I didn't know anyone, really, except for him. I wanted to get laid really, really badly, and I had a particular hard-on for this girl in our acting class named Julie. She didn't even know I was alive. But Rick fixed that. Women really responded to him, so he became good friends with this girl, constantly finding out personal stuff about her and kind of talking me up the whole time and sort of picking up on how she felt about me. And then he gave me a pep talk about calling her up. So, I finally went out with her, and even got her into bed, thanks to Rick. She turned out to be a real bitch and dumped me after only a couple of weeks, but if it hadn't been for Rick, I would probably still be mooning over her. You can't find a much better friend than that."

"That is so crass and inappropriate," Kari whispered to me. Yup. I looked back at the septuagenarians in our midst and wondered how they'd react, but they were just quietly watching. Ultimately, it didn't matter. Rick belonged to us, not them. This was our funeral.

Spanky knelt down beside the coffin in his fancy little suit, sobbing like a kid, and said, "Goodbye, old friend!" It was heart-wrenching just to watch him.

As Spanky returned to his seat, I reached out and patted his shoulder. When he got back to his seat, Maria kissed one of his cheeks and patted the other. The Funeral Director, who was standing by the door, flexed his feet and looked like he was about to move. It was now or never. I sprang to my feet and then moved quietly down to the front of the room. I studied the faces of the elders and of my friends, not daring to look into anyone's eyes. There were no expressions. People just wanted to hear it.

"There's not a lot I can add to what's been said, and said eloquently," I began, my voice quivering. "Like everyone's already said, Rick was a great friend. I was also honored to know him as a performer. He made my characters, like Mr. Slovenko, the Swinging Saberniaks, Billy from the Reverend Ridgelow sketches, just come alive." I looked up at the oldsters. Did they even know that he was in this comedy troupe? Did they have any idea who he was? I looked at Mr. Ratner for any kind of reaction. Not a smile, not a tic, not a raised eyebrow, nothing.

"But Rick was also a great friend. I have never seen anyone with such a great passion for books and plays and movies and even TV, and that enthusiasm was just infectious. And he was probably the most accepting human being I've ever met, in his own way. When my wife Kari first moved into the city, she was afraid of New York and afraid of my friends. Rick just immediately accepted her and put her at ease. The other thing I really loved about him is, with all he went through and all the anger that was inside him, he was never really mean-spirited. He channeled most of it into that outrageous humor we all know so well. And that's really all I have to say."

Once more I scanned the faces–the elders and even Mr. Ratner were blank and cold and dead. The other Chuckleheads and even Kari were just staring at me. But one face at the front of the room was beaming warmly. Jack.

After the service, I felt alive and happy again, as the spiritual weight of my own mortality had left me, at least temporarily. I sat there as people milled around Jack, and he slowly made his way in my direction. Finally, he stood right in front of me, and waited patiently until I stood and gave him a long, strong hug, without tears. "You know what I think?" he said to me. "I think Rick's up there looking down at us and laughing at us. Laughing at all this fuss we're making."

The Chuckleheads went to a nearby bar, where we got seriously hammered on sangria and regaled each other with all the Rick stories we didn't feel comfortable sharing at the service. It was exactly the gathering Kari and I had been waiting for.

"You know, sometimes when I think back about the troupe, it bums me out that it never really went anywhere," Dirk reflected at one point, after a couple of glasses. "But then I think, wow, what an experience to have had. Sometimes I think it's not even important where you end up. It's the journey that counts."

Wow, I thought: Maybe all those trips to Tibet had paid off after all.

Two hours later, pleasantly buzzed on a Sunday afternoon, we all hugged goodbye. Kari scratched Dirk's face and called him a sonofabitch because he'd stuck his tongue in her ear. And life was good.

ROB DINSMOOR